PACKMULE

CS-405: BOOK TWO

BLAZE WARD

KNOTTED ROAD PRESS

Packmule
CS-405: Book Two
Blaze Ward
Copyright © 2019 Blaze Ward
All rights reserved
Published by Knotted Road Press
www.KnottedRoadPress.com

ISBN: 978-1-64470-027-3

Cover art:

ID 20990394 © Nmarques74 | Dreamstime.com
ID 8814967 © Luca Oleastri | Dreamstime.com

Cover and interior design © 2019 Knotted Road Press

Never miss a release!
If you'd like to be notified of new releases, sign up for my newsletter.

I only send out newsletters once a quarter, will never spam you, or use your email for nefarious purposes. You can also unsubscribe at any time.

http://www.blazeward.com/newsletter/

The Jessica Keller Chronicles

Auberon

Queen of the Pirates

Last of the Immortals

Goddess of War

Flight of the Blackbird

The Red Admiral

St. Legier

CS-405

Queen Anne's Revenge

Packmule

Persephone

Additional Alexandria Station Stories

The Story Road

Siren

Two Bottles of Wine with a War God

The Science Officer Series

The Science Officer

The Mind Field

The Gilded Cage

The Pleasure Dome

The Doomsday Vault

The Last Flagship

The Hammerfield Gambit

The Hammerfield Payoff

Doyle Iwakuma Stories

The Librarian

Demigod

Greater Than The Gods Intended

Other Science Fiction Stories

Myrmidons

Moonshot

Menelaus

Earthquake Gun

Moscow Gold

Fairchild

White Crane

The Collective Universe

The Shipwrecked Mermaid

Imposters

EXPLORERS (JULY 1, 402)

It was odd that three weeks away would make her old ship seem like a foreign country, but Heather had spent most of June aboard the captured prize they had renamed *Packmule*. Coming back to *CS-405* was almost unsettling, by comparison.

But Phil had been adamant that the prisoners she wanted to interview remain aboard the Scout Corvette at all times, and he was in charge. Command Centurion Phil Kosnett, squadron commander. He was in his rights. Heather Lau was just a Senior Centurion, and normally Phil's Executive Officer, but she had breveted to command centurion when she took command of the monstrous freighter they had captured from *Buran* at *Laptev*.

And things were about to get a little crazy, out here so far behind lines in *Buran* space.

Heather made her way down the last hallway and opened the hatch to the main conference room. Phil was already there, along with Evan Brinich, who was taking over as First Officer while she was away, as well as Bok Battenhouse, the Boatswain who would figure so heavily into the next phase of the great plan.

Siobhan had brought Trinidad with her from the first prize, *Queen Anne's Revenge*. The crew had nicknamed the ship *Anna* from their transponder designation of *Anna's Vindication*. Siobhan's whole crew consisted of a couple of marines, an engineer, and a medic in Trinidad, Nakisha, Markus, and Max.

Heather had a much bigger vessel to command, but hadn't taken that many folks with her. Two Yeomen, Ryouichi Yamaguchi as a pilot for *Packmule's* insertion shuttle, and Galin Tuason to handle engineering. Three First-Rate-Spacers: Engineers Dedra Janowski and Zubaida El-Hashem, and marine Vlad Faurot. Everyone was working impossible hours with miniscule tools, but they were getting the job done.

The only other officer Heather had with her was Centurion Andre Gave, who had previously been the Chief Nurse under *405's* Surgeon, Kermit Hanley. Andre was still a little freaked out at being suddenly promoted to First Officer on a freighter, but Heather needed a medic as well as an officer, and *CS-405* had only shipped out with three dedicated medical staff, so he got elected.

CS-405 only had an official crew of two hundred and seven before three had died in the explosion that crippled the ship's JumpSails. With Siobhan normally over on *Queen Anne's Revenge*, along with four others, and the six people Heather had taken to *Packmule*, everyone else had to step up and learn new things.

Andre followed Heather into the conference room and

found a spot to sit on her right. He was reacting to shock by falling back on his training, nearly a decade ago since he had moved onto a nursing track at the Academy. Siobhan had promised they would all think like pirates soon, which apparently was a bridge too far for Andre right now.

But he was at least trying.

Heather ended up across from Siobhan, with Phil on the end next to a pair of open seats for today's guests. It was going to be a weird show, no two ways about it.

Phil smiled at her. He had always been a good commander, taking great pains to make sure his entire crew was well-trained and cohesive, but over the last two months, he had stepped it up another notch.

Seriously, one Corvette/Scout, the least-armed warship in the *Republic of Aquitaine* Navy, was single-handedly planning to take on the entire sector defensive fleet. Well, perhaps not take them on directly. Phil was sneakier than that. But they were making waves well out of scope for their tonnage.

"Ladies and gentlemen," Phil's gaze scanned everyone with a warm, hungry smile. "Welcome to Phase Two of the great invasion plan. Evan has found us a potential destination world, and I plan on asking our two guests a few questions today. I want you to pay attention to everything, and not share any militarily-sensitive information with them."

That got a laugh. Everything these days was top secret, after Phil had decided to stay put and do more damage in this sector, rather than successfully sail home with two stolen freighters.

"Questions?" Phil continued.

Heather shook her head and saw Siobhan do the same. Those would come later, when they needed to nail down the last few details and plan some raids.

The door opened a minute later and a marine escorted Phil Kosnett's two guests into the conference room.

Technically, Lan and Kiel were prisoners of war, but they were kept under minimum security most of the time. Siobhan's raider ship, *Queen Anne's Revenge*, had been their own little freighter *Resolute Revolution*, just five months ago.

Phil rose and gestured for them to take the last two seats at the table. They were dressed like civilians. All of their clothing and personal gear had been brought over and stored. And they would get it all back, one of these days, after Phil finally decided he had done enough damage to *Buran*.

"Welcome," Phil said after a few minutes to get settled and have some coffee. "We have gone through your extensive notes on this sector, and had a few questions. Everyone is here because it factors in to our current plans."

"Have we really become pirates?" the woman, Kiel, asked with a grin.

She was the more easy-going of the two. Heather had also decided she was the smarter spouse. Lan had been the pilot on their ship. Kiel had handled the engineering duties, as well as negotiated all their trades.

"Only on a technicality," Phil grinned back. "You have not enrolled into the *RAN*, and we have not pressed you into formal service, so you are my prisoners for now. But yes, the rest of us are pirates. *Lady Blackbeard* here is cutting a swathe of fear across the quieter parts of the *Altai Sector.*"

That latter aimed at Siobhan got a laugh out of everyone, including the two prisoners.

"So what grand evil scheme will we be compelled to participate in next?" Kiel continued in a light voice and a bright smile.

Phil's face turned serious now. Sober. The others fell into line.

"What do you know about the colony on *Abakn*?" he asked simply. "Your notes are almost blank."

"Middle of bloody nowhere," Lan spoke up, instead of his spouse. He was almost always quieter, so it was something of a surprise. "A standard colonial organization, with one city at the center, a few satellite towns on spokes, and rings of farms slowly fading to wilderness. We've never been because we can't make enough in trade for the time necessary to get there and back from anywhere."

"Nothing?" Siobhan asked.

"My spouse speaks truth," Kiel added. "The colony is only a century or so old. It was intended to be a launching point for other colonizing efforts in that region of space, before *The Eldest* pushed harder towards the *Fribourg Empire* instead. The world generally withered on the vine of irrelevance. While it might make a nice raid, I'm not sure anyone would even notice, when you seem to prefer notoriety."

Chuckles from everyone, including Lan. This was about as far from a military interrogation as Heather could imagine being.

"Heather?" Phil turned in her direction.

Heather put both hands flat on the tabletop and leaned forward a little as she organized her thoughts.

"You are aware that we captured one of *The Holding*'s primary sector food transports, yes?" she asked.

Both nodded, eyes much bigger than before. Capturing their little ship had been nothing. But there were only six of the big ships, running a dedicated loop around the *Altai* Sector, constantly moving food stocks between worlds. Most planets were largely self-sufficient, but the trade route allowed them to specialize, and then tiny ships like Lan and Kiel's could bring in exotics from other places for a nifty profit.

"I have been reviewing the logs and navigation records of that vessel as it walks the counter clockwise orbits to each of its seventeen stops," Heather said. "There are hints of some things we have been trying to get answers to, but it appears like the information is purposefully obscured. Possibly for the very reasons I am asking."

The two stared at her carefully, aware that what was coming next might not be all fun and games. The woman saw the trap, that much was obvious.

"Go on," Kiel prompted after Heather let the moment dangle.

"What does *The Eldest* do with Imperial prisoners captured at places like *Samara*?" Heather asked.

She found it fascinating that both spouses blinked abruptly and turned to look at each other simultaneously, puzzled, eyes down. Nobody had ever asked that question.

Lan's eyes suddenly lit up in surprise and shock. He focused on Heather and his mouth opened, but no words came out. Nerves overcame him a moment later and he clammed up hard.

"Lan?" she asked.

The man was grinding his teeth, but she couldn't tell if it was rage or embarrassment.

"Dearest?" Kiel leaned over and rested her head on his shoulder.

Tense moments passed as two different factions in the man's deep, brown eyes warred with each other.

Finally, he sighed and wrapped one arm around his spouse, kissing her on the top of the head as his eyes came back from whatever distance they had focused.

"It was well before you, dearest," he murmured to Kiel. "When I was very young and had just gone into space for the first time, a generation ago."

Heather remembered to breathe, and fought not to interrupt the man with questions.

"I was working on a medium freighter out of *Lena*," he mused distantly. "The next sector anti-spinward from *Altai*. We had to deliver a load of industrial, farming equipment to *Mansi*, because the original equipment for the colony had finally gotten too old to maintain, and there were no factories allowed outside the kremlin itself."

"*Mansi?*" Heather asked carefully.

"You won't find it in the records," Lan laughed raggedly. "It doesn't exist. We were told that. And that if we ever spoke of it again, we would join the prisoners down below nand never leave the planet again."

"Prisoners?" Phil probed.

"Aye," the man agreed. "Exiles. Except that I do not believe they came from *The Holding*, Director Kosnett.

The whole planet is an inverted prison. Prisoners are marched out of the main gate of the kremlin and forgotten. They must till the soil or starve. Several armed stations sit in orbit, watching for transmissions or ships trying to escape the atmosphere. Those are destroyed."

He turned to his spouse and smiled wanly.

"I remember the place so well because *The Eldest* had parked several old warships in high orbit, captured from someplace I had never heard of," he told her as he hugged the woman close. "I had always hoped to maybe sneak back and steal one when I got older. Before I found a way to buy my own and see the stars."

He turned now and picked out the three commanders of this little pirate squadron.

"Perhaps I am now a traitor," he mused. "But you have promised to send us home, one of these days, and even make us whole in the bargain. I do not believe those men ever got that opportunity."

"Can you find that world again?" Phil asked in a hard voice, angry at someone else.

"I can try, Director."

THE BACK OF BEYOND (JULY 18, 402)

Siobhan knew she would miss the little freighter, one of these days when they had to give it back, but she was truly enjoying sailing the wee beastie as a scout for the other two vessels.

Instead of the JumpSails that *Aquitaine* and *Fribourg* used, *Buran* had modern versions of the ancient JumpDrives that had given humanity the galaxy. You aimed at a point in space and threw yourself like a rock. Landing, you spent a while looking around, until you managed to identify your coordinates against your intentions, and then did it again.

For humans, an incredibly inefficient way to travel. Henri Baudin had invented the JumpSail so you no longer had to stop to check where you were. Just keep flying. *Buran* didn't care about the stopping, because all *The Eldest*'s warships were *Sentient*, controlled by artificially intelligent computers that could land and find their next jump within minutes, rather than hours it normally took a human.

But Siobhan was getting pretty good at galactic geometry, as filtered through the lens of gravity-zone interaction. And *CS-405*, while it had managed to repair the secondary JumpSails, still overheated them regularly and had to drop into RealSpace to let them cool, as well as reconfigure the matrix as the wobble got progressively worse every minute in flight.

Siobhan could outrun both Phil on *405* and Heather on *Packmule*, as a result. Plus, she was just another of the *Holding*'s light freighters, wandering the stars trying to make a profit, if anyone saw her. It made sense that she should be well out front, scouting. If somebody actually lived here, she could maybe bluff things, running away fast enough to warn the other two ships off.

But she hoped not. It was insane, the thought of stealing an entire planet. She wanted to be first.

Today, she was alone on her bridge. Trinidad, Nakisha, Markus, and Max were below and aft, doing whatever they needed to do to keep the ship flying. Siobhan just had the gray fuzziness of JumpSpace to keep her company, but she was almost to their destination.

It didn't have a name, the planet ahead. Just a number in the stellar cartography records they had merged from the three ships in the squadron. Nothing in any of their databases suggested that humans had been here in so long that it frightened Siobhan to even consider the scale.

According to the oldest records she had consulted, the era known as *The Terraforming* had begun some ten thousand years ago, and then lasted for at least a millennium as a concerted effort, with more terraforming on various local scales for another six thousand years after that. Right up until the *Sentient* systems almost managed to wipe out humanity.

This place was well and truly gone from everywhere else, more than eighty degrees of galactic arc from the Homeworld. So nobody might have seen these skies from the ground in five or eight thousand years.

"Emergence in four minutes," Siobhan said over the internal speakers.

Sure enough, the clatter of feet running this way. Forward on the main deck, up the stairs.

Suddenly, she had an audience. Max had gotten here first, probably waiting in the kitchen while Markus was all the way aft and the other two busy midship. Max was a skinny guy with blond hair. While he might tease her about skin nearly the color of coal, she had found a great counter, referring to him as *Oatmeal* occasionally. His skin was about the same hue. And everyone knew how much she liked to eat it.

But being first meant he got the left-hand seat and the others had to stand at the back of the tiny bridge and watch over shoulders. He grinned at her and pivoted the seat forward, careful not to touch anything.

Nakisha, closest behind him, got a smirk from Max over his shoulder as he turned away, so she walked up and leaned her forearms on his shoulders and her chin on the top of his head. If he moved too quickly, he would probably get one of her breasts smooshed into an ear.

Siobhan nearly giggled as the man realized that and turned beet red. He sat perfectly still. Trinidad chuckled from the door, but didn't say anything. Max was still a little shy around girls.

The countdown clock ticked the numbers down, and then they emerged into the universe again when the system hit zero.

She had gotten the hang of these drives. The last jump had been from the very outer edge of the system, when the local star was just the brightest one, but nothing special, and the few worlds just suggestions on distant scanners.

They had already eliminated one target on this path. It had been terraformed, but the star had cooled, or something. Much of that world had been locked into a serious ice age that covered most of the southern hemisphere and would play merry hell with growing seasons up north.

But now, they had dropped out close to the inner edge of the gravity well. There was a touch to it. And the ship had been tuned to far tighter specs than it had ever known, probably even straight from the factory.

A marble hung in the darkness before them. Mostly blue and gray, but with some big green spots as well. Life.

So far, so good.

"Initiating forward thrusters," Siobhan announced in a bigger voice than normal. "Nothing going to break back there, right, Markus?"

"Not on my watch, boss," the man rumbled back.

Siobhan grinned and plotted an insertion path into orbit.

It took her a few seconds to realize what it was that was making her nervous.

Every other planet they had visited in this sector

always had at least those same, four radio signals *Buran* always left in orbit for navigation purposes. One satellite on the exact north pole. Two more on the equator, ninety degrees apart. One small, fully automated station in orbit, filled with metal in bars, tubes, and sheets, plus a massive tank of water that could be used as fluid or broken down into gases as needed.

There was nothing here.

Even the path of radio beacons that *Holding* vessels used to navigate, the thing they called *Pochtovyi Trakt*, didn't come this direction.

Queen Anne's Revenge was well and truly in the middle of nowhere.

Siobhan set the ship to listening for signals and scanning the planet below them as her folks watched out the front port. She had inverted the ship so that they were watching the planet rotate above them.

"Now what?" Max finally breathed.

After ten minutes, any new planet got boring. Especially when there didn't appear to be anyone home.

At least, nobody with technology. Siobhan lived in slight terror that they might find an iron age culture, some lost civilization on one of these worlds. She really didn't want to do that whole First Contact thing.

Thank the gods that the records were accurate and nobody lived there.

"Now the rest of you go back to what you were doing, and I keep scanning this rock for signs of life," Siobhan answered.

They all filed out. With no immediate radio signals to listen in on, she had hours, and maybe days of survey work ahead of her. *CS-405* and *Packmule* were probably a day and a half behind her. Actually, they were probably still sitting quietly right now at the most recent rendezvous spot, ten light-years away.

Had this place been occupied, she would have either run at the first warning, or done some song and dance routine to escape and warn them.

Hopefully, there was nobody here.

FORWARD OPERATING BASE (JULY 20, 402)

CS-405 HAD GOTTEN THERE AHEAD of *Packmule*, but Heather wasn't surprised by that. She was still learning how her ship wanted to slide through JumpSpace. Which way it would drift in a hydrogen cloud. How sensitive the grav-sensors were for possible anomalies.

The other two ships were already in orbit when *Packmule* returned to RealSpace. This vessel also maneuvered like a small asteroid, so she had to take her time doing things, coming out at a greater distance than the two smaller ships and easing into a parking orbit.

Whoever built *Packmule* originally, designed her for a commander and a small crew of specialists to fly it, with a larger crew of stevedores and pilots doing most of the work below with shuttles and mover pods. She had one pilot for three shuttle craft, instead of six people. And nobody but herself to fly the main vessel right now, so she had parked Andre in the Director's seat where he could watch and relearn all the things he had worked so hard to forget as a nurse and not a command officer on the bridge.

She smiled at the thought.

"What's so funny?" Andre asked.

"Phil's always harping on about getting everyone cross-trained to work together," Heather said. "Don't think he ever got this far in his planning."

"The day I'm called upon to take over command of *CS-405*, it's going to be because I can't blackmail an Engineering Yeoman like Galin into doing it," he replied. "I'm a nurse, ya know. Not a ship-handler."

"Maybe we should fix that," Heather teased, ever so slightly, just to watch Andre's back come up, but whether out of fear or anger wasn't immediately clear.

Damned good nurse. Probably never fired a weapon in his life.

Hopefully, she could keep that streak alive for a while longer.

"*405*, this is *Packmule*," she said, opening a line. "Entering orbit now. Rendezvous in about three hours."

"Roger that," Evan's voice came back a few seconds later. "Think we've identified a landing zone in the southern hemisphere, on the smaller continent. You might want to prep your pilot. Siobhan's dropping out now to inspect from low altitude. If this is good, we'll drop the first box of supplies as soon as we can."

"Understood, Evan," Heather replied.

Instead of just calling the pilot directly, she opened the ship-wide intercom so everyone could listen in.

"All hands, this is the bridge," she said. "In roughly three hours, we may be ready to send the first two containers down to the surface, pending ground team. Plan your day accordingly and we'll have lunch in about ninety minutes."

She cut the line and turned to her First Officer. He was getting more confident in doing this, but she was planning on making things a little more complicated for him.

"You'll be in command while I'm gone," she announced with a grin at the horrified look on the man's face. "I'm leaving you, Galin, and Vlad, while I ride down to the surface with Zubaida and Dedra aboard Ryouichi's shuttle. Listen to Galin if he has opinions, and don't be afraid to radio, but you make the decisions from the moment I step off the deck, Andre."

Her response from the man was a heavy sigh. Honestly, if she had offered him a blindfold and a cigarette right now, he might look more enthusiastic.

"Just remember, we're the *Republic of Aquitaine* Navy, Centurion," she reminded him in a stern voice. "They're running scared of us right now."

"As well they should," he answered heavily. "We're plum crazy."

***

MOST *REPUBLIC* SHIPS carried simple administrative shuttles to move personnel and cargo around. Heather had made sure that she brought *405*'s primary pilot with her to *Packmule*, and then had the man spend all his spare time training how to fly the new kind of shuttle that *Buran* used.

The records called it an insertion shuttle, and it reminded her of nothing so much as a radically scaled-down version of *CT-9492*, the cargo tug that was assigned to Arott Whughy's *Forward Operating Monitor*. The size was vastly different, but both operated on the presumption of a long, skinny spine, with engines aft and a small crew section forward. In between were two spots where cargo modules could be attached on each side, like butterfly wings.

On *CT-9492*, those were full-sized cargo pods, while the insertion shuttle docked two of the largest standard transport packs *Buran* used: six meters by six meters by eighteen. They looked tiny, growing out of the belly of *Packmule*, but that ship was designed to carry two of them in a single silo, end to end, with twelve silos in a single row across and one hundred and eight rows front to back.

She had a few larger pods in the ship's belly, a full silo deep by four silos square, but no way to move them to the ground. Fortunately, those were carrying bulk liquids and grain shipments, so she could eventually empty them into smaller transport packs by hand. The squadron still had nearly a year and a half of food before they had to start worrying.

Heather was riding in the co-pilot seat, above and behind Yeoman Yamaguchi as he backed out of the flight hangar. They had loaded the shuttle up in deep space at the last laager, when Heather could bring over a whole mass of experts to handle those big boxes safely.

Now they were going to land them and maybe create the beginnings of a farm. Because if you want to go crazy, how much weirder could it get than to steal an uninhabited but viable planet behind enemy lines and set up an illegal cattle ranch?

Heather glanced at the other two passengers, Zubaida and Dedra. This shuttle could hold six, and she was about to go get the other two off of *CS-405*.

"*CS-405*, this is *Saddlebags*, departing *Packmule* now," Yamaguchi said with the slightest superiority. "Let my passengers know so I don't have to hang around for them all day?"

Heather chuckled. It didn't matter what they flew. Pilots would be pilots the galaxy over.

"Roger that, *Saddlebags*," Evan called back a moment later. "Two for transport."

Ryouichi had gotten quite good at his task. It helped that the shuttle itself was programmed to be easy for anyone to fly, assisting the pilot by compensating for the load. The first two containers going down were mostly camping and building supplies, rather than bulk food, so they were flying light. Later loads would get interesting.

Docking took all of three minutes. Ryouichi didn't even shut the engines down, so much as idle them as he opened the hatch to the crew space.

Heather laughed again when she saw the two of them approach. Bok Battenhouse was the oldest sailor she knew, sixty-two years Standard with nearly forty-two of that on active duty. Even old-timers usually retired after thirty, but Bok claimed he wanted to see sixty years in, just to teach the young punks how to do the job right.

And he was a great teacher. Plus, he was *405*'s Boatswain, the senior enlisted man on board. That didn't mean as much in the *RAN* as other places, since so many

Yeomen took the step to Centurion rather than Chief, but Bok had never wanted the responsibility of a commission.

The Chief was short and broad, like he had been carved out of an oak tree stump. His companion, on the other hand, was his opposite in just about every way possible.

Able Spacer Avelina Indovina was a tall, skinny woman, towering over Bok by at least ten centimeters, but she was all bones and whipcord. And young. Bok claimed he had shoes older than Indovina, which wasn't a great stretch, since the Spacer was barely twenty-one.

But the tall brunette, with long hair always pulled up into a severe bun, had also been raised on a cattle ranch, similar to Bok, and still had a civilian veterinary medical certificate she had gotten from a local farmer's organization back home as teenager.

Both carried field backpacks as they boarded, stowing them overhead and finding seats.

"Ready for an adventure, you two?" Heather asked as the shuttle took off.

"I offered her Missus Battenhouse," Bok said with a laugh. "She suggested Mister Indovina instead."

"Although," the young woman volleyed back as she settled in. "Now that I think about it, I'll be up in the main house and you can stay down in the barn, at least until you manage to build yourself a bunkhouse or something."

That got a laugh. It was good. The two of them would be alone on the surface for a while when everyone else left, getting ready for a future that might never come, if something went wrong.

Heather kept her face neutral as her subconscious

insisted on listing all the possibilities, the least frightening of which involved these two as Adam and Eve in a forgotten paradise.

Hopefully, there were no large predators or weird diseases on this new planet.

The shuttle ride down was sedate, if Heather had to pick a word. The systems were designed to bring cargo to the surface without damage. In a pinch, it was apparently possible to program one of the shuttles to fly itself reasonably well. A crewmember just sat in the seat and made sure nothing went wrong.

The planet below was Earth-like, in the way the Homeworld supposedly had been, in the time before. Mostly ocean, with about a dozen continents of various sizes arrayed in odd patterns as things moved around. Their target was in the northern hemisphere, a medium-sized continent that was more or less attached to a larger one, divided off by a wall of mountains running north and south as the two slowly ground together. South, another continent was just far enough away to create a calm, almost inland sea, with only three outlets to the wider, world-spanning ocean.

Saddlebags was coming in from the south, across a small mountain range covered with an alpine forest. Heather had been born a city kid, but the place looked lovely.

Scanners picked up *Queen Anne's Revenge*, sitting close to the shore of a long rift lake that bisected a valley. From the scale, it had to be around twenty kilometers wide in most places, and perhaps two hundred long, but the mountains on all sides formed a solid rim over four thousand meters tall in most places.

Isolated. What Bok had specifically requested. An island, except land-locked. Bok had explained that he didn't know a damned thing about boats bigger than the kind he could row around a pond, so it would do him no good to be on an ocean shore.

Heather wondered if she should suggest a more interesting advanced survival training program, when they got home. There were enough inhabited planets out there, but few people other than specialist marines could probably survive living rough for a long period.

But how many people were as crazy as Phil Kosnett, to even suggest something like this?

She turned to Bok and Avelina, watching them as they stared out a window. Low murmurs flowed back and forth between them, but they sounded good.

"Thoughts?" Heather raised her voice.

Both of them looked back at her, then each other. Bok shrugged and nodded to Avelina.

"Assuming fish in that lake, and tools to make a boat, we should be good," the young woman said. "Island effect should reduce the size of any large animals likely to be running around, and I can set traps for the little ones."

"We'll still need to thin the big-game predators a little, presuming there are any," Bok added. "Then we should be able to let stock run loose for the most part. Make sure to steal me a half dozen horses, so I don't need a ground vehicle all the time."

Heather nodded and added that to the list in her head. Avelina would be training folks how to handle large animals and supervise them in space, while she and Bok stayed here to establish the first buildings of what the man was calling *Lighthouse Station.*

Seriously, a cattle ranch as a forward operating base behind enemy lines. But the Fleet Centurion had wanted crazy.

They landed just upslope from the other freighter and debarked into a cool, cloudy afternoon. This area was a huge meadow, possibly caused by flooding from spring runoff drowning trees, or something.

Big area, a kilometer long and a third of that wide, mostly composed of tall grass and shrubs, with bigger trees in every other direction. Birds overhead appeared to be looking for critters scared off by the bigger birds. Or maybe just curious. Everyone was armed, just in case.

And Markus Dunklin, Siobhan's favorite redneck engineer, was holding a thing he described as a shotgun. Metal stock shaped for a shoulder. Round tube nearly three-quarters of a meter long, and big enough for two of her fingers to fit inside. Apparently, it used a chemical reaction called gunpowder to fling a thumb-sized cylinder of ball bearings at a target. The other version fired a slug of lead with a steel core, supposedly proof against big cats.

Heather checked that her pulse pistol was charged, safe, and accessible.

"What's the season?" Avelina was asking the redneck engineer.

"Late spring, local," Siobhan replied instead. "Not much axial tilt, and no moon overhead. Evan Brinich figures that we won't see more than about fifteen degrees temperature difference across an entire year, up here. Plus, the mountains funnel weather in weird ways, so it will be lots of drizzle, year around, but probably not heavy snow. Of course, never going to be all that warm and sunny, either."

"About like home," Avelina observed. "What about the lake?"

"What about it?" Siobhan asked.

"Fish?"

"How the hell would I know?"

Avelina turned to Bok and motioned he and Markus closer.

"So I need to do some fishing," the tall woman said. "One of you could help, so it goes faster."

"Take Markus," Bok said. "I need to site things for the landing pad, then figure out where we want the shipping containers, and then where the rest of the buildings will go."

He turned away from them and gathered the rest of the people together as Heather listened.

"*Queen Anne* has that damned repulsor truck for moving containers around, which is good," he growled, thinking out loud now that he had touched the earth himself. "Long term, a dozer of some sort would be good. Maybe a full tractor, with a back hoe and tools to drill a well. We can run pipes down to the lake and bury them, for now. Same with a septic tank and a drain field."

"So this place meets your needs, Chief?" Heather asked the obvious question.

"Ask me tomorrow," he replied. "But we'll make it work."

Bok looked around at the dozen or so people in a loose circle.

"I need to take a hike in a big circle with Trinidad and Nakisha," he gestured to them. "Dedra, you come with me. Zubaida, you supervise putting the boxes here and there, in an L-shape, upwind and uphill, respectively, with the main side accesses facing into a quad we'll stomp down with as many feet moving around as we can. Heather, can you call *405* and get me as many people as Phil and Kam can spare?"

Heather took a step back and tried to envision things as she relayed the message to Evan in orbit. Getting the ball rolling.

Too many moving parts right now, but she didn't need to do anything but be a strong back helping unpack the containers when they were placed for now.

Lighthouse Station was going to become a thing, very soon.

CAMPAIGN, PHASE TWO (AUGUST 17, 402)

THE SHIP HAD FELT ALMOST derelict, with so many crew off-ship over the last month. Most of them were down on the planet, setting up the depot that Bok was going to turn into a forward base when the ship left. Another group were aboard *Packmule* right now, getting that ship ready to start rustling cattle.

Literally.

Phil stared around the conference room on *CS-405* where so many of his plans had taken shape. Not much to look at, just off-white walls, a wood conference table, and heavy-duty tan carpeting, but all the craziness was contained in these walls, perhaps just waiting to bleed out and infect the next crew, after the First Lord had him Court Martialed and grounded permanently.

The only question in Phil's mind these days was if that would happen before the new Emperor of *Fribourg*, the former Centurion Wiegand, gave him a medal, or after.

Today's meeting was going to be a small one. Nobody really needed to be involved except Siobhan and Heather. Evan was just here because he was acting First Officer with both of his bosses off-ship being pirates.

And cattle rustlers.

The hatch opened and Evan came in first, followed immediately by Heather and *Lady Blackbeard*. Heather hadn't earned a crazy, piratical nickname.

Yet.

He had no doubts there, either. She'd have one before this was all done.

It was interesting, watching the tableau as they all sat. He and Evan in uniform on this side. Both of the ladies dressed up like civilians, even here, across from him.

"Are we there?" Phil asked.

He didn't need any preliminaries. Not with these folks. They had been building to this for months, since he first announced his plans to try to top Jessica Keller's *Long Raid*.

"I have only one question," Evan asked. "Do we have everything set, in case we want to actually steal the orbital station over our target?"

Siobhan grinned, as he expected. Heather's smile was absolutely predatory. It was frightening to watch her emulate *Lady Blackbeard*. To learn from her.

Hopefully, they would both have bright careers remaining, after the Navy was done burying him under the jail.

"We opened up enough space by setting four containers down on the surface," Heather said. "The other four got dismantled to make the parts we needed for everything else. Can't slide it in on the rails that are there, but we'll only need a few hours of work. Setting it in place here will actually take much longer."

"And the rest?" Phil asked.

"That depends on what we find on the ground, Phil," Siobhan said. "Same as *Barnaul*, there will be a significant element of random chance involved. If we can sneak in and around, I can get Bok everything on his shopping list. If not, we might have to take what we can get and move on to another target. I'm okay with pillaging down the entire Atlantic Coast of Central America if we need to. Lots of birds with one stone."

She was *Lady Blackbeard*. Her crew had taken his own words and twisted them into an operational vocabulary, and brought everyone else along. Staying in the fringes of the *Altai* sector was Central America. Crossing over into the *Lena* sector was raiding North America. Heading back across the *M'Hanii Gulf*, going home, had become *Sailing to Portsmouth*.

Phil nodded.

"Very good," Phil decided. "Get everyone off the ground who's coming and we'll depart in sixteen hours. I've laid in a sailing plan that gets up to *Abakn* in good time. If the place follows the standard pattern, we'll be dealing with no orbital defenses worth mentioning, and the only issues we'll have will be on the ground."

"How do we get a gunship?" Siobhan asked. "Anything besides *405* with any weapons?"

"If we didn't need a full shipyard to do it, I'd be

tempted to sacrifice one of the turrets here and mount it on *Queen Anne*," Phil replied grimly. "It's possible we could attack one of the larger planets to try and take one, but then we run the risk of armed stations and missiles. Not worth pursuing right now. Our mission is to set things on fire and force *Buran* to chase ghosts all over the frontier. Which brings me to the last point. The prisoners."

Everyone grew serious, watching his face. Lan and Kiel were always referred to as *Guests* and treated as such. The twenty-seven former crew of *Packmule*, the survivors, were not. They were locked up and fed regularly, but had no intelligence value, so no reason for Phil's crew to interact with them.

"When we are done on *Abakn*, assuming success, we will transport them to the surface near our target and turn them loose," Phil explained in a severe voice. He sounded like Tomas Kigali in his own head, which was not the comparison he wanted today, but it couldn't be helped. "I have considered asking Kiel and Lan about relatives or friends that might be recruited, but we have no way to easily contact anyone, let alone transport them as a work crew. However, we will be undertaking to survey for the planet *Mansi*, according to what Lan was able to remember, so actionable intelligence on missing Imperial prisoners of war will be second priority, behind stocking the ranch for Bok and Avelina. Questions?"

They didn't have any. Too many unknowns, this far away from their target. The problem was, once they got close, there probably wouldn't be any time to organize things.

The fog of war frequently turned into the chaos of battle.

Especially with Phil Kosnett trying to set the entire *Holding* on fire.

LIGHTHOUSE STATION (AUGUST 18, 402)

"You missed your chance to escape me," Avelina said with a smirk as she walked out of the shipping container that had been serving them as a house up until now. At least the ground crew had finished building them a nice, two-story house with eight bedrooms, and windows made of transparent metallic alloys.

Bok looked over at Avelina and gave her a good, stern appraisal. To make a point, at least in his own head, he had dug out a pair of field boots that he had owned for four years longer than this young woman had been alive. Three times resoled didn't count. He had still bought them twenty-five years ago.

It grounded him. Reminded him of one of those fanciful, non-existent Hometowns that everyone liked to carry with them when they left.

"Guess I'm stuck with you, Indovina," he replied after a beat. "You sure you wanted to volunteer for this mission? You might be stuck with me for the rest of my life."

She stuck her tongue out at him, which somehow just seemed to fit. On anyone else, it would have come across as juvenile, but she never slipped out of a mode that seemed three parts cowgirl and one part sailor. Reminded him of girls he had known back home.

Bok turned his eyes back to the sky, and then the clouds, the mountains, and the lake they had named Ladaux. Lots of fish in there. Weird variants of things he knew from other worlds, but all of it edible. Some ungulates in the valley, mostly deer that had sized up and down in scale, in response to the isolation. A few predator species that were solitary cats of various sizes. Nothing like coyotes or wolves. Just cats.

Had no fear of humans. Not yet. He would have to change that, given time. Still knew how to stalk things, a skill he'd never really lost from being a kid. Bobcats and cougars, back home. Roughly the same here.

With twenty hands to do the work, they had built a nice little ranch station here. Pens big enough for a variety of domesticated creatures to be held. Big barn for keeping things dry and safe. Motion and thermal sensors around the outside of the range, adapted from the ship, to warn if one of the cats got too close. Repulsor bikes to go out and deal with them when they did.

He looked forward to horses, if that was possible. Bikes required recharge time on the auxiliary power generator in container number two, so he couldn't go too far from home right now.

"Lev for your thoughts," Indovina asked, standing silent next to him.

Not lurking. Just watching.

"Sorry for the poor city kids," he answered honestly. "Never get to see something like this."

"Didn't we both join the Navy to escape something like this?"

"Everybody's escaping something," Bok said, mind and eyes wandering.

The cleared landing zone that could accommodate both *Queen Anne's Revenge* and *Saddlebags* at the same time. The covered-over water-pipe trench up from the lake bringing fresh water. The field churned up, well off to the side, where the septic tanks were pumped the drain field.

He turned, feeling rather than seeing Indovina turn with him.

Two shipping containers on the left, stacked up with a ladder connecting them inside. A third one perpendicular. The fourth one well off to the side, storing some of the equipment that he would need to level trees, split them, and take care of a ranch and farm.

The farmhouse itself could hold all visitors. If Siobhan brought back hands, he could turn them loose on building a bunkhouse.

"What were you escaping, Bok?" she asked, pulling him back to the present and then casting him deep into the past.

"Who," he corrected.

"I assumed that," she said. "We all have a who."

"Nobody and everybody," Bok replied cryptically. "Found out she and my best friend had kinda forgotten to tell me some things. Decided to run off and join the Navy instead of beating him to death."

"Ouch," she said. "You loved her that much?"

"I was nineteen," Bok said. "We all do stupid shit at that age. Everything is of utmost importance. All turns out to be a pile of beans, when it comes right down to it."

"Ever talk to them again?" Avelina asked.

"Her a couple of years later," he reminisced. "Home on leave between assignments. He'd run off with a bartender by then and left her with a daughter. She was trying to go back to school and find herself."

"Him?"

"Nope," Bok grimaced. "Standing offer to kick his ass if I did. Figured it wasn't worth looking. You?"

"Almost verbatim," she laughed. "Are we all dumb, crazy punks?"

"We are, Avelina," Bok laughed with her. "But it let me see the galaxy in ways those folks never imagined. Hell, I'd retire out here if I could."

"Why not?" she asked.

"In the middle of *Buran* space?" Bok turned sidelong to glance at her.

"Sure," she said. "If Keller wins, this might all be fair game. Planning to file a request with the Imperial Throne to be made the Duke of this planet. Big boss. Even if we get chased off later, it'll still look damned good on a resume."

Bok laughed and laughed at that.

"What?" she demanded. "What's wrong with asking?"

"I think that it's a magnificent idea, Your Grace," Bok finally got the giggles under control, until he saw the crestfallen look on her face, then he started up again.

"Duke Avelina Indovina of *Lighthouse Station*," Bok

pronounced grandly. "Remind me to file paperwork for a ducal grant of land. I want this whole valley."

"You can have the southern shore of the lake, from the line at both ends," she laughed back. "I want to put a summer palace on the north shore so I can sit on a patio and watch you peasants sweat to make me rich."

That triggered another round of laughter, that ended in a silence like a blade dropping, for no reason either of them could name.

"Are we nuts, Bok?" she asked, serious this time.

"The best kind, Avelina," he replied soberly. "The best kind."

ABAKN (SEPTEMBER 4, 402)

"So what do we do if the bad guys show up in the middle?" a voice intruded on Siobhan as she worked the scanners.

She turned and appraised Max, standing in the door to *Queen Anne's* bridge with a hangdog look. He didn't have much to do on this ship, being the medic, so he ended up doing a lot of scut work, mostly cleaning and cooking, all the while hoping that they never needed his skills.

Must be a rough way to make a Lev.

Siobhan patted the left-hand seat as an invitation to sit and talk. She had to act like a Command Centurion today, guiding her charges and taking care of the emotional and psychological well-being of everyone.

How Phil managed it and kept sane she hadn't yet figured out, but her crew were a better-balanced fit.

As Max sat, she pulled the scanners back a little and set the screen on the console between them to show as much of the system as *405* had managed to scout from clear out here on the perimeter.

"We do whatever we can to ensure the safety and escape of *CS-405*, and then *Packmule*," she replied in a serious voice. "In that order. We are the least valuable, and most expendable part of the squadron, because Heather has all the food and Phil has responsibility for everyone."

"Whatever?" Max asked in a voice filled with awe.

She forgot sometimes that the young man had his soft and vulnerable side. Everyone who had to deal with Max professionally got the hard-ass medic who charged in and fixed people, regardless of their opinions on the topic. Even stubborn folks like Markus had learned to back down when Max was working.

But this was the guy stuck in back with no clue what the big players had on the table.

"Whatever," Siobhan repeated. "Anything we have to do to make sure the others get home safe. Whoever we have to kill included."

"Are you really that ruthless?" Max asked.

"Max, if the only way out involved taking *Anna* and ramming a Hammerhead so that *405* could make the edge of the gravity well, the only question would be if the rest of us could manage to abandon *Anna* first, or if we went down with her."

"And that's what it means to be a pirate?" he asked.

"That's what it means to be an officer, Max," Siobhan corrected. "To be the *Republic of Aquitaine* Navy."

A chirp sounded from the boards as Max fell silent. She could tell he was a little overwhelmed, but she knew he needed the truth up front, all hard and ragged, so he could process it and make it his own. Max was like that.

She turned to the board and pressed a button.

"*Queen Anne's Revenge*," she said aloud. "Go ahead *405*."

"Feeding you an orbital file now, *Blackbeard*," Evan's voice came back over the line. "Standard four signals in orbit right now. Can't tell much about the surface detail from this far away, but I've incorporated Lan and Kiel's ideas on a planetary colony. Phil wants you and Heather to digest them, and then we'll swap in crews and make a run down there in twelve hours from now."

The three ships were hiding out at the edge of the solar system, like they always did when going someplace. *CS-405* had the best scanners in the galaxy, and Evan had tuned them to paranoid levels, so Siobhan was fine with him scouting for everyone for now.

"Roger that," she replied, cutting the point-to-point laser connecting the two ships.

It was far better than radio, when you needed sneakiness.

Shortly, *Queen Anne's Revenge* would be on point, leading the others in. Hopefully, nothing more than a simple surface raid.

She turned back to Max. He had regained some animation and he stood up, nodding.

"You tell the others," Siobhan said. "Everyone runs through a sleep cycle now, and then we'll eat dinner in ten hours."

"Yes, sir," he replied, leaving her on the bridge.

Siobhan stared at the scanners, as if they could tell her what to expect below, but the galaxy was keeping her secrets today. At least there were no ships of any kind in orbit right now.

That would make the first part easier.

STUNT DUDE (SEPTEMBER 5, 402)

JUST LIKE AT *Barnaul* and *Laptev*, Trinidad had all six of his people with him today, plus nearly twenty more crew, down in *Anna*'s cargo hold. Not much for a planetary invasion, but more than enough for a raid. Bok wasn't with them, and Kam was back up on the ship being Chief Engineer, so Galin Tuason had taken the old man's place with the raiders, rather than staying up on *Packmule* with Andre.

Anna couldn't really function with this many crew aboard, getting in each other's way, but they only needed to run down and disable the target, so that *Saddlebags* could land with two specially configured containers.

It would be his job to get in and keep the locals contained while the crews went to work. Hopefully, this would be more like *Barnaul* was supposed to work out, rather than the messy eventuality they ended up with.

"All hands, stand by for landing," Heather's voice came over the speakers. "Ninety seconds to ground."

He had been expecting Siobhan, but she was probably busy actually flying the ship through the darkness of night on *Abakn*.

They hadn't even been challenged in orbit, according to Siobhan. Just noted by automated systems on the station, and then nothing.

Trinidad was furiously hoping that *sleepy* applied to this colony, and not *death-trap*. They had been lucky so far, but it was a manufactured luck, not something he wanted to trust.

Trinidad turned around and counted noses. Until Heather and Siobhan came down to the cargo deck from the bridge, he was in charge.

"Markus," he called. "Mount up and make sure the truck's ready. Everyone else, grab your packs and get ready."

Mild grumbling from the non-marines, unaccustomed to backpacks filled with survival gear. His marines just laughed at those folks, when they only had to carry less than five kilograms each. He and his routinely ran up and down every flight of stairs on *CS-405* with a twenty-kilo training pack, just to stay in shape.

The ship canted suddenly, pushing everyone forward that hadn't been paying attention, and then settled on to the ground with a lot of bangs and crunching. Even as light as *Queen Anne's Revenge* was, and as good a pilot as Siobhan was, it was still a lot of mass moving around.

Engines powered down aft and the internal lights and fans came up to full power from the lower level they had been on approach. Trinidad pushed the button to lower both fore and aft ramps. According to Evan Brinich, they were in early spring at this latitude, and another late snow was expected.

As the ramp dropped open, a chill wind suddenly cut through everyone, from the bitching and whining. Again, not his marines, who had listened to the entire briefing and closed up their jackets and pulled out hats and gloves before they landed.

Everyone else hurried to join the smug marines as Trinidad walked down onto the surface of a new planet, reveling in the shallow footprints he was leaving in the snow.

"Fall in," he yelled, pretending to be a proper officer and all that. It sounded good, anyway.

A mob trundled down and joined him off to one side, backlit by the bright lights inside the landing bay and the exterior floods on the hull itself. A few moments later, Markus Dunklin fired up the big repulsorlift truck they had stolen on *Barnaul* and eased it quietly down the ramp.

Unlike most of the crew with him, the marines had combat helmets with some serious built-in electronics, so he called up a map and checked distance and topography. They had landed more than thirty kilometers from the nearest farmhouse, and even then had come down to the deck and flown several hundred kilometers below the horizon, just to get here quietly.

Around him, Nakisha Onks had her original helmet, as did his only security Yeoman, Teresita Riechs. She was the one he had left in charge, back on *405*, while he was off having adventures, and she had done a good enough job that she would probably be his peer as a Centurion pretty soon.

Heather and Siobhan came down the ramp a few seconds later. They had two of the remaining helmets with all the stuff built in, and his folks wouldn't be that far from someone connected.

Trinidad counted noses again and checked the charge on his pulse pistol. Nervous habits.

Everyone accounted for.

"You ready?" Siobhan asked as she got close.

"Just waiting for you," Trinidad replied.

"Mount up," Heather called to the group, walking over to the truck and climbing up inside.

It would be a tight fit, with her and Siobhan crammed in next to Markus, but they needed to be warm and out of the nasty wind that would come up when the truck got moving.

"Remember," Trinidad yelled over the grumbling. "Backs to the front of the vehicle, except marines on watch. Keep your packs on to block the wind, scarves tight, and heads down."

The bed of the truck was designed to transport a six by six by eighteen meter container, one of the standards that *Buran* used. There was a one-meter-tall gunwale around three sides, mostly to hold a box in place. It wasn't solid, but it was enough to generally shelter people.

Trinidad dropped his faceplate down and locked it. Nakisha and Teresita were already ahead of him. He put them on the two front corners and took a back one himself, with Vlad and Gerry opposite him. Wil and Little Jim were riding in the middle for now. They would swap out with Vlad and Gerry in twenty minutes or so, those four not having a helmet with a heater built-in to offset the wind chill of the night.

Trinidad glanced up, but the sky was a wall of clouds, a slightly lighter gray than the ground. *Abakn* had a couple of smaller moons that didn't do much to light up the nights on this planet, even at full face.

No, this felt like the kind of place where folks rolled up the sidewalks at dusk, put the kids to bed, and then read by firelight for an hour or so, rising with the damned chickens in the morning to milk the cows.

Trinidad could hope.

"*Stunt Dude*, you're up."

The words broke through the reverie that had descended on Trinidad as the truck had slowly wended its way through the trees. At one point, they had even flown over a creek, following it a while to get closer, and now they had reached the point that the two women in command had decided was close enough.

The truck was grounding as Trinidad checked his pistol once again.

Wil and Little Jim piled out the back and took up positions on the flanks before Trinidad even got to the ground. Vlad and Gerry were a moment behind them.

"Strike team, form up forward," Trinidad said in a loud enough voice.

He strode to the front of the truck and joined his six people, plus Heather and Siobhan.

The lights were off here. Markus had one of the

helmets and used it to drive in the dark, so hopefully nobody but the owls knew there were pirates on the planet.

Everyone was armed on this mission, which meant stunners for everyone, plus pulse pistols for his marines. Nakisha carried the rocket-grenade-gun Markus had dreamed up, but wasn't supposed to use it without specific orders. And he could generally trust her discretion.

But at the same time, only he and his people were trained in combat. They would lead, bringing Heather along, while Siobhan waited here with the rest of the crew to come in once the building was secured.

Everyone was expendable down here, but the marines were more expendable than the rest.

Trinidad checked the map on the inside of his faceplate. They should be just over a small hill from their target, and about a kilometer straight-line. It had started snowing again, but this was a fine, soft drift, without much weight or wind driving it.

Back home, his dad had referred to this kind of weather as a footprint of snow. Just enough that you could mark it, but not enough to make life miserable.

Of course, there were already about eight centimeters on the ground here, and the weather didn't look to get above minus five anytime soon, but that would work in his favor. People would stay indoors, hopefully.

Clock said they still had about three hours until sunrise, so hopefully nobody was awake over there.

Trinidad counted noses again. It was something of an obsession, but it calmed him. Shortly, it would be time for

Lights! Camera! Action! and he needed to have everything prepared.

There would only be one take, so it had to be perfect, special effects and everything.

Working on a tight budget, B-film again.

"Any last minute thoughts?" Heather asked.

She was technically in charge of this part of the raid, but he had talked with her extensively about what was coming, and she was happy to stay a little back and let his folks expert the hell out of this. They were getting to be pretty good at the job of pirates, although his mother would wail with indignation at what her youngest son had turned into.

More than normal, that is. He could have been a doctor, or a lawyer, like his older siblings. Instead, he had become an actor, and then a marine.

Now, piracy.

"What's so funny?" Heather asked, looking at the grin on his face.

"What am I gonna tell my Momma?" he said with a grin.

"Mine thinks I play piano in a cat house," Nakisha laughed. The rest joined in.

It was an old joke. Anything not to tell her you joined the Navy.

"Nothing here," Trinidad said. "At this point, we just need to get a clear view of the target and assess the next steps."

"You've got point," Heather said.

"While you're walking, we'll have a quick potty break here, and then mount up to come to your rescue,"

Siobhan promised. "Try not to do anything too embarrassing."

"Who?" Trinidad was hurt. "Me?"

"Gerry," Siobhan turned to the biggest marine present. "Make sure you get it on camera."

"Aye aye, sir," Gerry even saluted, while everyone else laughed, but Trinidad was *Stunt Dude*.

As the saying went: *he could have been an actor, but he wound up here.* And he was still kind of an actor, depending on how you looked at it. And this was just another stage.

"Move out," Trinidad grumbled, once everyone stopped giggling.

He and Nakisha had point. Teresita and Heather were in the middle. Wil and Little Jim had the rear. Wil was a big guy, strong and tough. A recruiting poster kind of marine.

Little Jim, on the other hand, was the absolute minimum, both in height and weight, for a male marine. He was, however, as mean as a weasel when it came to violence. As crazy as Nakisha, but even more deadly. Anyone trying to sneak up on them tonight would be sorry they even got out of bed in the first place.

Top of the hill. Trinidad found a fence.

Damned good thing it was snowing, or he would have walked into it, but there were four lines of ice-cold running horizontally on his thermal sensor. With barbs. And the top one was a double wire, with an inner one isolated by plastic arms, so an electric current could run through it.

He didn't feel like checking to see if it was live.

"First barrier," he said aloud, crouching down and waving the rest to join him.

Beyond the fence line, and down in the hollow spot below, a series of warm spots stood out against the cold. From the size, he guessed cattle, but he wasn't about to go wake them up and check.

He could see the front of the main building from here. Two stories, with a porch that wrapped all the way around the outside, from this vantage point. No lights were on in windows right now, but the porch had one, as did something on the back, out of sight.

Off to his left, a long, skinny barn, similar to what they had built for Bok and Avelina, back at the *Lighthouse*, so Trinidad tentatively assumed horses. Not his problem, as there were a couple of crew back with Siobhan that claimed to understand the beasts.

On the right, a low building that covered a lot of ground, but was only one story tall. From the smell, maybe a barn for the cattle to come in for milking.

The building he wanted was on the far side. A barn just like artists drew when they wanted to say *farm*. Dutch colonial roof and all. Red walls faded and worn. Big sliding door on the near end. That would hold some of the equipment Bok had tasked him with procuring, hopefully.

Even with light amplification, the snow made a mess of distance vision, so Trinidad flipped a coin in his head and went left. They could cut through a pasture with cattle, as long as they gave them a wide berth, but he was looking for a road or a trail that could skirt them.

He got lucky, maybe.

The field with the cattle was fenced off, and a roadway

circled the bottom of the hill. Ruts looked to have been cut by wheels and reinforced by hooves, giving them a path to follow.

Nakisha's arm on his stopped Trinidad cold.

"Dog," she murmured.

"Where?"

An arm came up and pointed to a small building off to one side. He had thought it was a chicken coop or something, until she pointed it out.

"Little Jim," Trinidad turned and said quietly. "Dog needs to go to sleep."

Unlike Nakisha, Little Jim didn't revel in violence. He just got the job done. And the mutt would most likely survive. That wasn't a given had he sent Nakisha down there.

Instead of taking Wil along, the weasel tapped Gerry on the shoulder and the two of them moved like black ghosts across the white field.

Trinidad made a note to plan more uniforms for future raids. His brain had said night raid, so everyone was in dark clothing. But everything here had a layer of snow on it, reflecting a little light, so dark things stood out. He would need probably two more color schemes in the future. Something white for alpine ops, and something a neutral gray-green that would fit into shadows. And maybe something tan color, for a place like the valley where *Lighthouse Station* was, with all those grassy meadows scattered around.

Gotta have a bigger wardrobe budget.

The air was still and calm. The light snow falling was more like confetti in a parade than anything else. Trinidad watched his two ghosts slide forward along the edge of a fence, until they settled.

Snow muffled the sound, so if they fired a stunner, nobody heard it up here. Hopefully nobody down there, either. After a few seconds, they moved closer and settled again. Trinidad really needed to pee from all the adrenaline coursing through his system right now, but it could wait.

Finally, the two figures separated and closed slowly with the building.

Gerry turned and flashed a pocket light in their direction once. Silent and effective. Either the dog house was empty, or one of those shots from a distant angle had been effective.

The dog was hopefully safe. Trinidad didn't mind hurting people in his vocation, but the dog hadn't asked for it.

"Move out," he said quietly, standing and following his two marines into the front yard.

The doghouse made a good enough amount of cover from most of the house, so Trinidad gathered everyone there.

Let's see, first unit director over there. Secondary cameras there and there to pick up action shots like snipers. Bad guys like us charge this way. Heroic defenders move off that way to escape and call the police to save them.

Trinidad chuckled a little too loud.

"What?" Heather whispered.

"I think I already made this movie once," he said.

"About five years ago. Almost the exact, same setup, except we don't have repulsor bikes and flamethrowers."

"Markus can probably fix that," Nakisha observed dryly.

And he could. Crazy-ass redneck engineer was just itching to build new toys.

"Okay," Trinidad said. "I'll take the front door with Wil and Little Jim. Teresita, you have the back door with Vlad and Gerry."

"What about me?" Nakisha huffed.

"You and Heather are the backstop," he said. "Anyone getting out of the building is likely to go for a vehicle in the barn. You stop them from getting in there."

"And if we can't?" Heather asked.

"Then I shoot them down," Nakisha patted the grenade-rocket-gun fondly.

Trinidad nodded.

"What if they get a horse instead?" Heather asked.

"Then it's an entirely different movie," Trinidad said to quiet laughter. "Move out."

He watched the front of the building for any movement, any lights, while the others got right up against the side of the building, below the level of the windows. The house had eight steps up to the front door, so the bottoms of the windows were about four meters up. As long as everyone was quiet and unseen, they could do this.

"Little Jim, they likely to lock the front door in a place like this?" Trinidad asked as the others disappeared around the edge of the building.

"Doubt it, boss," the man shrugged. "But I'm sure that they can drop a bar inside that will stop anything but Nakisha from getting in. Cheap insurance against something like a bear deciding he wants in. If it was summer, I'd expect upstairs windows to be open, and we could climb up and get in that way. You and I could, anyway."

"Anywhere you can go, I can manage," Wil rumbled with just a hint of defensiveness.

Trinidad smiled. They were always competitive, his marines. Made them better soldiers.

"You take the door," Trinidad told the weasel. "Wil, you've got the right flank. I'll take the left. Just waiting for the signal from Teresita."

As if on cue, his helmet beeped once. Nothing more than that, and over as quickly. Anyone awake had to be on the right frequency and paying attention, and even then all they would get would be that meaningless beep. But it told him enough.

"Go," he whispered, rising.

Little Jim went up the front stairs like a ghost, possibly not even leaving footprints in the snow, but Trinidad wasn't going to take the time to check. He and Wil were noisier, about as loud as a church mice, by comparison. Everyone had a stunner in their hands.

The weasel turned the knob on the door without pushing it in more than a quarter inch. He looked back and nodded to indicate that he could get in. Trinidad nodded back. He could see better in the dark, with all the electronics in his helmet, but he figured that maybe put him on a par with Little Jim.

The door opened on silent hinges and they flowed inside, to Trinidad's first surprise.

He had been expecting an interior like you always saw in a Western.

Big salon for entertaining guests. Dining room for family and hands. Grand staircase up to the bedrooms.

He kept forgetting this was *Buran, The Holding.* They didn't do it that way around here. Children were separated off at birth and sent to training crèches, probably in the city.

The room he was looking at was a dining and recreation area like he might have built for marines on a ground assignment. It did have a flight of stairs up, but there was no carpet anywhere in sight, just polished hardwood floors worn by a lot of feet and a big, common room, thankfully empty and with nightlights at shin level providing some modicum of light.

No, not empty.

Snores emanated from a corner.

Little Jim was there in a heartbeat. Stunners made remarkably little sound, and the snoring stopped.

A wall separated them from the back of the building. Trinidad moved close and listened. The door was on a pivot, rather than hinges, reminding him of a restaurant.

He took a chance on the comm.

"Teresita, common room in front," he said quietly into the radio. "Door to the kitchen I'm guarding."

"Kitchen in back," she replied. "Cleared. Coming through that door now."

Trinidad stepped back as the door cracked enough to

reveal his Yeoman's helmet and her gun. He grinned and motioned her forward.

"Thoughts?" she whispered as she flipped her faceplate up and came through, the other two in her wake

"Bigger cast than we expected," he smirked. "Lots of extras working for day wages and no Screen Actors Guild card."

She nodded.

"Upstairs?" Wil said. "Feels like a barracks here."

"Probably a big, open room filled with stacked bunks," Little Jim said. "Space walled off for officers, showers and head probably down a whole wall. Or would they do two?"

"One," Gerry, of all people said quietly. The big, dumb marine? "*The Holding* is done in common, so they won't gender the facilities. You aren't allowed to mate without permission, but sex is acceptable, within limits. Probably an even gender split upstairs."

"Weapons?" the weasel followed up.

"Assume *Packmule*," Trinidad said. "Officer will have a weapon, and probably keys to an armory with long arms for dealing with stock and predators. Everyone ready an assault grenade, in case we have to soften the place up."

"Boom stick?" Vlad asked.

"No," Trinidad said after he considered it for a moment. "I need Nakisha keeping everyone bottled up here. Wil, you've got the best arm. If all hell breaks loose, put your grenade into the officer's quarters. Follow it up with a frag if you can't get close enough to use your stunner. He'll have the radio, as well."

Nods. Serious faces. A small assault against a single

family with kids and hired hands, all easily controlled, might have just turned into a small riot.

"Jim and Wil on point," he said.

The stairs up were along a wall, with a railing around the top, tucked into a corner. That left them out of the way, and several of them could look up into the main room on the second floor at the same time.

Six stacked pairs of bunks. Door to what looked like the head. Another door at the far end, closed.

Little Jim held up a hand to pause everyone on the stairwell. He pulled off his scarf and wrapped it carefully around his gun hand, indicating to Wil to do the same.

Yeah, that made sense. Maybe silence them completely.

Trinidad waited for the two men to move, and then gestured everyone else up to where they could see. And pour fire and chaos into the room if they had to.

Little Jim and Wil would be in the middle of it, but they were marines. It came with the signature on the page.

Most of the bunks were filled. Someone up here snored almost as loud as the man downstairs had.

On the snore, Little Jim and Wil both fired, taking out a top and bottom bunk.

Trinidad had his eyes, and his gun, focused on that closed door at the far end.

The pair moved to a second stack and zapped the people, covered by the snores.

A third pair of locals went down just as steadily. Trinidad relaxed, just a might.

Maybe they could pull this off.

"Wha…??" a muddled voice spoke up. "Hey!"

Crap, someone had gotten up to hit the head in the dead of night. Little Jim spun around, but Teresita had already nailed the woman standing in the doorway.

She went down heavily, and the snoring stopped abruptly.

"Now," Trinidad said in a normal voice.

Little Jim moved like a ballerina. Wil was his clumsy shadow, by comparison.

Vlad and Gerry poured fire into the last set of bunks. The angle was bad, but anyone too close to an edge would get brushed. If they sat up, they were toast.

Dead silence. Adrenaline rush. Trinidad really had to pee now.

Trinidad raced up the last few steps, leading the rest of his team. A signal to the point pair had them listening at the door to the officer's bunk, so he took Gerry and Vlad and cleared the head. Silence abounded.

Nobody home, but a damned fine time to use the facilities. Vlad waited until he was done, and did the same.

Back in the main room, they approached the last door.

"Locked but silent," Wil whispered as he got close.

"Kick it in," Trinidad ordered.

Time was burning.

Gerry shattered the doorframe with a kick, and Little Jim was inside before Gerry was done rebounding. Trinidad heard two quick shots from the stunner and then a muffled curse as Little Jim stomped out.

"Could have used grenades and she'd have never noticed," the weasel opined.

The stale reek of alcohol followed him out.

Trinidad peeked in. One woman on the bed. Two

empty wine bottles on the floor on their sides. Fog of drunken stupor emanating from every surface.

Yuck.

"Zip tie everyone," Trinidad ordered, before switching channels. "Heather, building one is cleared. We'll be down in five to clear the rest."

He didn't bother waiting for her response. He was too professionally offended at the drunk officer. Wanted to kick her, but that wouldn't solve anything.

He'd settle for robbing her blind.

DAWNLIGHT (SEPTEMBER 5, 402)

ELEVEN PRISONERS. Six horses. Seventy-three chickens. A little over nine hundred head of cattle, spaced out in various pastures, pens, and fields. Two tractors. Nine vehicles, from zip bikes up to a wheeled, flatbed pickup truck for hauling hay rolls, complete with the spiked hydraulic system on the back to lift and lower the massive bales.

Heather nodded to herself as she closed down the computer system for the ranch and looked around the office of the woman who had been in charge of the facility.

Squalid. Hadn't been cleaned in ages, with empty candy bar wrappers wadded up everywhere. Plates stacked on the edge of the desk with food dried on. An arms locker that had contained one pulse rifle and nine bottles of wine locked up in it before it got emptied.

She understood Trinidad's anger, but also understood that the woman was in charge of a cattle station in the middle of nowhere, on a planet more or less forgotten in an abandoned colonizing effort.

The ultimate dead-end job. Some people couldn't handle that. This woman had apparently been one of them.

"Heather," Trinidad was in the doorway. "You need to see this."

He was gone before she could ask, but he wasn't running, just moving out of her way, so she stood and joined him. The bound prisoners had been moved downstairs, into the big common area, where several people were guarding them at all times. No food or drink this morning, and one potty break under guns had kept them contained.

Being outnumbered by armed, angry gunmen had done wonders to keep them quiet.

Trinidad led her through the kitchen and out the back door, to where Nakisha and Vlad had two of the prisoners separated from the rest. Both men. Late twenties, maybe. Possibly over thirty.

The closer one had skin a darker red than the average member of *The Holding*. Hispanic, perhaps, mixed with a few other things.

"Identify yourself," Trinidad ordered the man.

"Flight Lieutenant Granville Veitengruber," he said in a calm, serious voice. In English, rather than Mongolian. "IFPN-12576-9JD5JC4. Most recently attached to IFV *Germania*. Shot down and captured at *Samara*, Imperial Founding Year One-Seventy-Two."

Oh, shit. A real prisoner of war? Here? Why would you put one on a farm in the middle of nowhere?

Because there was nowhere for him to run. It made a twisted sense. How many of the miners at *Barnaul* might they have missed?

"Senior Centurion Heather Lau," she introduced herself. "The war with *Aquitaine* is over, Lieutenant, and we have made common cause with *Fribourg* to fight *Buran*. I am the First Officer of the Corvette/Scout *RAN CS-405*, flying under IFV colors."

He looked dubious, but that wasn't a surprise.

"Much has changed in the last eight years, Veitengruber," she continued. "Among other things, we're looking for prisoners like you that we can rescue and take home."

She could tell he expected it to be a trap. A trick of some sort. His teeth ground for a moment. The man surprised her by turning to the other prisoner.

"Tell her," he said in Mongolian.

This man was smaller. Perhaps not even Heather's height, whereas the Imperial looked to have several centimeters on her. The second stranger's skin was a golden brown that was almost bronze. Brighter than normal for *Buran*. Darker than the Chinese Diaspora.

"Indeed?" the man asked in a quiet, tenor voice.

Veitengruber nodded. Once. Fierce.

"My name is Malondenishk Abarantakratar," he said in a musical voice. "I was born in the nation known as *NovLao*, and captured by the *Invader's* forces five years ago."

"Where is *NovLao*?" she asked in an apprehensive voice.

"As I understand it from Granvie, the far side of *The*

Holding from the *Fribourg Empire*, madam," he said with a nod.

Granvie?

"I can't promise to get you home, Sri," she explained, shocked. "But I can rescue you from here."

"And if we choose to remain?" he asked.

"Why in the world would you want to do that?" Heather was perplexed.

"I cannot return home," the Imperial said, almost defiantly. "Will not, without Deni. But I would not be welcome in *Fribourg*. We would not be."

Oh? Oh.

Heather growled, but only in her head. Yes, the traditionalists would not welcome that sort of a relationship. Back home in the Empire, such behavior, even between two consenting adults, was, at best, ostracized, and frequently criminalized.

She could see the new Emperor changing that, eventually, but it probably wouldn't do those two any good in the next generation.

Still…

"We are an *Aquitaine* warship, Lieutenant," she fired back at the man. He had never had a female commanding officer, until he came to this world. The drunk wouldn't have warmed him to the idea. "On an extended raiding mission, deep into *Buran* with no plans to return to Imperial space anytime soon. Until then, nobody cares, except how hard you work. You will not have to return to *Fribourg* afterwards, but you do not have to stay here. But if you desire to remain a slave, I won't stop you."

Probably never had a woman talk to him like that,

either. Not that he was probably that interested in females to begin with, given the circumstances.

"Oh," he said. "Really? We could be free?"

"Yes," she said. "And my commander will be quite interested in hearing about other cultures, even five thousand light-years away."

"Thank you," the smaller man, *Deni*, replied.

Veitengruber had fallen mute.

She turned to Nakisha.

"Have these two help out with the field teams when *Saddlebags* gets here," she ordered. "Then make sure they're on *Anna* when we lift."

"Yes, sir."

Heather smiled at the two men.

"Welcome aboard, gentlemen."

RUSTLERS (SEPTEMBER 5, 402)

Siobhan laughed to herself when nobody was close by.

I did not join the Navy to steal cattle, but I also never expected to be a pirate, either.

They couldn't steal all the cattle. For one thing, they didn't have enough hands to keep them taken care of on the flight to *Lighthouse Station*. Additionally, they didn't have anything like a container to keep that much beef penned during the flight.

What Markus and friends had done was take four of the big containers and rebuild the interiors. Six by eighteen was a reasonable floor space, and they had added a catwalk overhead that someone could stand on to drop hay and feed to the big creatures below, without risking getting kicked or trampled.

Milking was going to be a pain in the ass, but that wasn't her problem. Each container would simply be landed aboard *Packmule* and use the big ship's gravity to keep the cattle happy. Others would go in and milk the critters.

And rather than try to mess with the grav-plates on the ship, Heather had just had Yamaguchi fly each of the three shuttles down, loaded with two containers each, and haul off three loads of cattle. A fourth would carry six of the horses and all the chickens. The last two were in the process of being loaded with a tractor and all its implements, plus all the vehicles and milking equipment that could be moved.

Talk about inducing chaos along the frontier. She could already imagine her image showing up on the vid for this week's episode of *Dangerous and Wanted*.

Heather walked over to the tree where Siobhan was leaning, watching growling sailors carry dismantled gear towards the shuttle. They had already run the leftover cattle off into a distant pasture.

Siobhan watched expectantly, but Heather just stood nearby and watched, with the same, goofy grin.

"You heard about the two prisoners?" Heather asked after a bit.

"Did," Siobhan agreed. "What do you think Phil will do?"

"Depends on them," Heather observed. "If the one is really a pilot, then we've suddenly got two to fly insertion shuttles on raids. Not sure how we go about rescuing more of them, other than just keep our ears open when we take prisoners."

"Thinking about *Barnaul*?" Siobhan asked.

"How many men did we leave behind there?" Heather

nodded. "Even if we had no idea they might be available to be rescued."

"Maybe organize a prisoner's revolt?" Siobhan's face turned sober. "Let them know that the war is getting closer?"

"Won't work," Heather shook her head. "We don't know where we're hitting next, and sure as hell don't want them knowing. Plus, we're not likely to come back, so the best we might do is get them killed for no reason. I wish we had the ability to land on a planet and hold it long enough to find all our people and get them out."

"What about the alien?" Siobhan pressed.

"Deni's human," Heather countered. "But yeah, we've got another one like the Khan of *Trusski* on our hands. Makes me wonder if Phil might not decide to blast lengthwise across the entire *Holding* to see who lives over there and how we could help."

"Sounds like something Tomas Kigali might do," Siobhan murmured.

"We're all a little crazy," Heather replied.

Both women's comms beeped at the same time. Siobhan was faster to pull hers out.

"Skokomish," she said. "Heather's with me."

"Trouble might be coming," Evan said quickly. "Picking up a flyer headed in a direct line for your location from the city. ETA fifteen minutes. Nobody else in motion, and no radio traffic I can pick up. How close to ready are you?"

"More than fifteen minutes," Siobhan said. "Keep a watch on everyone else, in case they decide to send reinforcements."

"Will do," the man said, and then the signal was dead.

Heather whistled to get heads turned this way. Trinidad and Nakisha came at a hard jog when she waved. In fact, she started jogging towards them, Heather in tow.

"Company coming," she said, loud enough that everyone could hear. "Finish loading, but all the security marines find hiding places. We want them to land, so act friendly and wave, but pretend like the radio system is completely dead and nobody knew about it here. Heather, you pretend to be in charge. They'll be expecting a woman boss. Hopefully, they've never met her. Veitengruber, you run interference."

Siobhan joined the seven marines in finding hiding places. The rest of the men and women went back to work, loading equipment up the low ramp into the insertion shuttle's container. They wouldn't have it locked down well, and there was no way to hide an insertion shuttle on the surface.

They would just have to play it by ear.

"Nakisha," Siobhan yelled in the direction of the big barn where the marine was. "Be prepared to shoot if down it they refuse to land. Everyone else, total radio silence from here on in."

A hand waved back.

Within moments, calm had settled on the big pasture. The tractor and the truck were loaded. The big tanks to hold milk were partly dismantled, but not ready to go. From her hiding spot, the crew were going after the refrigeration and pasteurization equipment. Tanks were just sheet metal bent and welded. New ones could be built easy enough later on.

Siobhan found herself checking her pistol again and grinned. Trinidad would be on his fourth or fifth time doing the same thing, but he needed that to calm his nerves. She popped her knuckles instead.

A sound overhead caught her attention. Flyer coming in. Not at a dead sprint, like a strafing run. Not a slow orbit to see what the hell was going on and maybe open fire from overhead.

Nope. Neighbors coming over to see what the hell was going on and why nobody was answering calls.

Everyone on the ground waved, all friendly like. And there were only a half-dozen bodies out there, rather than twice as many pirates as this farm had hands.

Siobhan had ended up over inside the dog house. Rather than listen to the beast howl and bark constantly, or keep having to stun it, Heather had locked it in the commander's office upstairs, where poop and piss on the floor would probably be an improvement.

Still, it gave her lots of cover, separated from the rest of the team. And a flank she could turn, if she had to.

The flyer orbited once, nice and calm, and then flared forward and started to land.

It was built rather like the truck they had stolen, a big passenger hauler box that rode on repulsors, but it was smaller and leaner, looking rather more like a goose in flight than an armadillo someone had tossed into the sky.

The port hatch had been open when it flew, but the craft landed with the starboard side facing her. Siobhan could see a pilot in the right-hand seat, with a side window open to let in air, even as brisk as the day was.

It landed on skids tall enough that Siobhan could see

someone jump down on the far side and stalk over to where Heather and the two locals were waiting. Two more sets of legs appeared, but didn't stray far. Probably two guards that wanted to stay close to the warmth of the ship, rather than follow the boss over and get mud and snow all over their boots.

Siobhan studied the craft. No guns were obvious, and the pilot was looking the wrong way. Executive decision time. Her folks were close enough to departure if nobody had come with the locals as backup.

She crept from inside the dog house and moved closer to the craft. It had a cantilevered wing across the top, probably to help with lift when it got up to speed. It also cast a shadow in the midday sun. There were portholes on this flank, but hopefully everyone would be looking at the action over there.

She was staring hard at the pilot. Or rather, the back of his head as he watched the action on his left as well. No mirrors on this side for him to glance back, so he would have to turn his whole head to see her.

Ten meters. Eight. Six. His head came back to center and started to glance this way.

Siobhan burst into a run, right at him with her stun pistol in hand. For a moment, the man's eyes got big in shock, like he couldn't even imagine what was going on.

Then the gun in her hand registered.

He looked down and powered the bird for flight.

Siobhan stopped thinking about how crazy this might be, and stepped onto the skid next to the pilot, grabbing a handle on the outside of the door and centering her weight, just as the man pulled the control stick back and suddenly the flyer was airborne.

Without thinking, Siobhan stuck the stunner into his window and shot the man dead center. He fell as far forward as his seatbelt would allow.

Unfortunately, his hand fell against the controlerss at the same time, and the flyer suddenly leaned over to starboard, still lifting, but now threatening to turn turtle with her under it.

Very much not good.

Siobhan saw sky through the windshield as she was hanging straight down. Her one hand turned to a deathgrip. And she wasn't sure if she could grab the skid with her toes through steel-toed boots, but she was damned sure going to try.

The stunner went into her holster, and then she reached up and grabbed the open window like she did this stunt every day, and twice on Sundays.

She knew how to fly something like this, but needed to get it under control before it crashed.

Or Nakisha decided to put a rocket grenade into the bay.

Siobhan stabbed a hand in and pulled the stick more or less upright. The controls were more tricky, but she found a big, friendly button blinking in the center of the console in front of the stunned pilot.

Autopilot.

She mashed it with a fist and held on for dear life as the craft suddenly pitched to port and nearly dumped her out of the sky.

Okay, hovering. Good. Everything is zeroed in.

She sucked a hard breath down, pulling the freezing air into her lungs like fire, and pushed the stick forward gingerly, still hanging from the side of the aircraft like a lunatic spider.

Slowly, the craft agreed with her and descended. Siobhan shifted her feet around on the skid as ground came up to meet them. Cattle began to stampede madly away as they looked up at the terrible Roc about to pounce on them from above.

Contact.

In the cockpit, the autopilot beeped happily and began to shut the craft down.

Huh. Good, solid programming. Assume something bad happened to the pilot and the craft needed to listen to a panicked passenger, and then take care of them.

Siobhan was in the middle of a pasture. She found the handle to open the door and pulled. The pilot was easy enough to detach, so she pulled him out and dumped him for now.

Glancing into the passenger bay, a pair of huge eyes stared back at her, attached to a young woman who was the color of the snow outside.

Crap, missed someone.

Siobhan quickdrew her stunner and aimed it.

"Understand me?" she asked in a voice juiced with adrenaline and cold.

The passenger nodded.

"Undo your seatbelt and get off the craft," Siobhan continued. "Anyone else aboard?"

Quick headshake no. A broken bobblehead doll.

The woman managed to unhook her harness on the

third try, and slid across the bench, standing in the midday sun on shaky legs. Siobhan went around the bow of the craft and joined her.

They had flown almost two hundred meters before landing. Things looked to be under control over there. Markus was tearing across the field in the big truck, with Trinidad and Nakisha in the bed, when Siobhan looked around.

The truck grounded heavily and skidded forward. The two marines were at her side in a beat.

"Trying to take my job?" *Stunt Dude* asked as he covered the new prisoner.

"Hey," Siobhan replied. "If you were out there doing the crazy shit, I wouldn't have to now, would I?"

That got a laugh. Almost hysterical in tone, but humor was good.

Join the Navy. See the stars. Become a pirate and a cattle rustler.

It was time to get off this rock.

PRISONERS (SEPTEMBER 5, 402)

HEATHER HADN'T PLANNED it this way, but hanging around with pirates was apparently rubbing off on her. At the first sign of trouble, she had drawn and shot the short, fat man who had stomped over to talk to her. Her second shot had hit one of his bodyguards, but that man was already unconscious, the target of three other bolts.

Now she had him tied to a chair on the front porch of the farmhouse, snow and crap all over his expensive-looking uniform from where he had face-planted. Gerry was keeping guard with a stunner drawn. They were going through plastic restraints at a prodigious rate, but those were replaceable.

Siobhan had brought along from the captured flyer a young woman who was apparently the man's secretary.

Or whatever euphemism they used for it on this planet. Beautiful, curvy, and apparently about as smart as a box of rocks.

Heather seriously doubted her skills at shorthand.

Overhead, Evan checked in every five minutes, but nothing was moving that he could pick up with a regular hard ping of the surface. Somebody was probably getting a beep in the middle of their songs, depending on which frequency the Science Officer was using.

"Thoughts?" Siobhan asked in Bulgarian as Heather ruminated.

It was a language nobody but crew would understand.

"How close to loaded are we?" Heather replied similarly.

Short pause as Siobhan looked back over her shoulder.

"Probably, we could go now, if we had to," *Lady Blackbeard* said. "In thirty minutes, we won't have to repack things in orbit."

"I'm feeling antsy," Heather observed. "Pushing-luck-time. We should bail."

"What about the prisoners?"

Heather stepped forward and tapped the man on the shoulder.

"Gerry, bring this one along on *Anna*," she ordered.

The man nodded and pulled a long knife out and slid it in between flesh and zip tie with an expert's touch.

"Any particular reason?" Siobhan asked.

Heather noted that she was more interested than concerned.

"Chaos," Heather replied. "We've gone beyond simply robbing planets of gear and property. Now we're holding prisoners for ransom. We can drop him on our next target. Speaking of which…"

She pulled out her comm and checked a countdown clock. The prisoners they were going to drop here would be on the ground in twelve minutes. That sounded like a good time to swap the twenty-seven coming down for one going up.

"All hands," she said into the local comm. "Fifteen minutes to departure."

The man Gerry was escorting was awake and moving stiffly, but in an obvious panic to be around strangers speaking a foreign language.

"Be calm and we'll eventually release you," Heather said in Mongolian.

His head snapped around at her words, but he seemed to relax.

Heather smiled at him, but it wasn't particularly friendly.

This one was just another pawn in Phil's *Great Game*.

FREE (SEPTEMBER 6, 402)

THE ONE STRANGER was a tall man, lanky and somewhat forgettable. Brown hair that needed to be clipped soon. Nervous but hiding it reasonably well in Phil's estimation.

Of course, to be aboard an *Aquitaine* warship was probably a worst nightmare for a man like Veitengruber, once upon a time. Now, he was in the process of being rescued. Or something.

Phil turned his gaze to the second man. Malondenishk Abarantakratar. *Deni*. Shorter than the pilot. Golden-brown skin that seemed to glow. Short, black hair. Fierce eyes.

The two men sat as close together as the conference table would allow, with Heather on the far right and Siobhan on the far left and four marines in the room with him and Evan.

"So your craft was disabled at *Samara*, and you were taken prisoner," Phil repeated to the Flight Lieutenant. "Eventually, you ended up at *Abakn*, where you were expected to serve the greater cause of *The Holding* by doing manual labor on a cattle farm."

Veitengruber nodded. It hadn't been a question. He was still waiting for that shoe to drop, from the look on his face.

"Is this standard practice?" Phil asked. "There have been many ships lost at *Samara* over the years, but nobody knows what happens to them. Because *Buran's* ships self-destruct when defeated, the *Empire* has never been sure they ever took prisoners. I presumed they did, based on what the defector told us."

"Processing took about four months, from what I could tell at the time, Captain," Veitengruber said. "Then I was rounded up with around fifty other men and shipped off. At each stop, a few men were separated and vanished. I left about in the middle, so there are more in whatever direction they went from here."

"You are currently still in the *Altai* Sector, Lieutenant," Phil explained. "That's the one directly across the *M'Hanii Gulf* from the *Ural* Starbase at *Samara*. We're headed into a new sector to continue our raiding, after we drop off all the loot at our local base."

"And what is to be our fate?" Deni asked in a polite voice still crafted from steel.

"What would be your preference?" Phil asked simply. "I understand from Heather Lau that you do not believe you would be welcomed home as a hero. The *Empire* has changed radically, but I agree with the sentiment that some changes will require more than our lifetimes."

Veitengruber nodded, but remained silent.

"As commanding officer in the field, I have a great

deal of latitude," Phil continued. "We are headed to a world we call *Lighthouse Station*, where all the cattle and chickens will be delivered to a ranching outpost, along with the milking equipment. With that in place, the limiting factor on my squadron becomes wear on the parts, some of which are not replaceable with equivalents from *The Holding*, so eventually we will need to return home."

Phil studied the two closely.

"You could return to ranching, if you desired," he said simply. "The planet currently has a known population of two. You could also take up arms aboard my squadron. We are operating under a *Fribourg* flag for now, but we are still the *Republic of Aquitaine* Navy. And you do not need to make a decision today. We would like to ask other questions, if you are up to it?"

"How may we help the war effort, Captain?" Deni asked.

"Knowing that there are prisoners in penny packets, we can add a rescue effort to our campaign," Phil said. "But our major limiting factor right now is firepower. This is a scout corvette, and the least-armed warship class in the fleet. Both freighters are completely unarmed."

He left the rest dangling.

"All of Buran's warships are *Sentient*," the Imperial observed after a moment. "So stealing one would be impossible. What else is there?"

"He means our old ships, Granvie," Deni leaned over and murmured quietly. "Captured Imperial and *NovLao* vessels that might be intact and could be stolen, correct, Captain?"

"Indeed," Phil said. "Plus anything either of you might know about a planet known as *Mansi*."

Veitengruber shuddered involuntarily at the name. Deni reached out a comforting hand and grasped his. After a moment, it slid under the table where nobody might notice.

Phil didn't care. Neither did anybody else he knew. People with minds that small and closed didn't last long in the Navy. Either they grew up or they shipped out.

"We were occasionally threatened with that name," Deni said after a few moments. "Like the boogieman your parents might invoke if you were bad as a child. Behave, or we'll send you to *Mansi* and nobody will ever hear from you again."

"I see," Phil said. "We think we have a location. Or rather, three target systems from which we will begin our survey."

"Yes, but those are bodies of men," Deni said. "You'll want a graveyard, instead."

"A what?" Evan spoke up suddenly, leaning forward to inject himself into the conversation.

"*The Holding's* warships are alive," Deni said, waving a hand as Evan started to counter. "*The Eldest* treats them as living creatures. Captured warships are thought of, spoken of, in the same way, so when ships are no longer useful, they are sent to cemeteries."

"Old freighters taken out of service are dismantled and recast," Evan said.

"That is my understanding, yes," Deni answered. "But *The Eldest* does not desire the secrets of foreigners to be discovered, at least according to threats and intimations cast upon me by my captors. So the ships are sent to cemeteries. Perhaps your records will show such?"

"Crap," Evan said with a nod to Phil. "Cultural miscommunications. Thank you, I will go back and start my work from scratch."

"How soon until you return to the Empire?" Veitengruber spoke up in a small voice.

"Months, at the very least," Phil said. "Jessica Keller has taken command of this frontier, but we were separated. Almost as lost as you. After her last great raid, she will need time to rearrange her forces on this border, so we are in the process of causing as much trouble as we can behind lines. *Buran*'s fleet is not much larger than *Aquitaine* or *Fribourg*, for many more worlds, so they have to thin themselves out to look for us, but at the same time they must maintain local superiority of firepower, so they cannot just send a single Hammerhead to every world, lest they stumble into Keller and she annihilates them. It is into that chaos that I have chosen to stick my blade."

Both strangers nodded. As did his three officers.

"We will reconvene later," Phil announced. "Go rest and eat as free men. The war will wait."

HAY STACKS (SEPTEMBER 8, 402)

Evan stared at the charts like he could make the computer give up its secrets by psionic brute force. It had stubbornly resisted him for two days now, but that was no surprise. Combining three radically different datasets into one always required some level of guesswork. Something had been missed, or misidentified.

In the end, he had gone back to the original data from *Packmule*, spinning up a new navigation database on a small computer system and installing the records there. Searching was slower this way, but progress was progress.

A door chime brought Evan back from too deep inside his head.

His cabin wasn't a mess, but could have been cleaner. A plate from dinner he hadn't had time to haul off to the wardroom. A notepad with a dozen pages folded over the top, filled with notes that were fast turning into meaningless doodles as nothing jumped out at him.

Evan ran a hand through his blond hair and reached a

hand out to open the hatch. Company right now was probably a good idea, all things considered.

He was not expecting Phil to be standing in the door with a rueful look on his face.

"You look like hell," the command centurion said as he entered and closed the hatch behind him. "When was the last time you slept?"

Evan stopped and tried to do math. The number he came up with was not a good one.

"Too long," he replied, surprised at how exhausted his voice sounded.

"Thought as much," Phil nodded. "You don't have to solve it today. We're still four or so days out from *Lighthouse Station*, and we'll be there for probably a week, just unpacking things and settling everyone in."

"It's there, Phil," Evan said ,onviction underlying his tones. "I haven't found it, but that's because the computer keeps throwing too many false positives and I have to spend too much time tracking them down and eliminating them."

"Change your parameters," Phil said in a voice that wasn't *quite* an order. "You're trying to find a needle in a haystack."

"That's what this is, Phil," Evan countered.

"No, actually. It's not," Phil smiled gruffly. "Eliminate anything not in *Altai*, *M'Hanii*, *Samara*, or *Lena* sectors, right off the bat. I have no intention of going any farther afield than that."

"But that's…"

"As far as my campaign goes right now, Brinich," Phil overrode him. "If our target is outside that range, we're probably better off running all the way home and bringing back Jessica. You've been trying to identify the entire *Holding*, haven't you?"

"Well, yeah," Evan said, somewhat sheepishly. "And I've found all sorts of useful intelligence, but not a stellar graveyard."

"Good," Phil continued in a voice that Evan squirmed a little at. "Then, eliminate any system that doesn't have orbital navigation warnings."

"Every system has junk, Phil," Evan countered. "Asteroids, comets, moons. Something."

"Yes, but for most systems, those don't rise to the level of threat," the command centurion said. "You're thinking of this like a Science Officer, and not a pilot."

"Huh?"

"Pilots only care if something is going to get in their way, or if they have to avoid a certain area," Phil said. "Such as a forbidden zone where enemy warships are laid up for salvage or intelligence."

"I've been wondering about that," Evan said. "Would they keep them? Or toss them into the nearest star or maybe crash land them on a planet?"

Phil finally moved deeper into the room from the hatch, taking a spot on the foot of Evan's bunk, the green blanket tucked in tight and squared away.

"If I was in charge, I would have kept at least two of every class of thing we captured, or as many parts as could be salvaged," Phil said.

"Why two?" Evan was confused.

"To make sure that the one was a standard design," Phil said. "And not some random one-off captured and of no real intelligence value. Every time I caught a new version, I would probably discard the oldest remaining one, on the theory that new ships would have incremental improvements."

That made sense, and Phil had been doing this for far longer than Evan had. Hell, this ship had been Evan's first assignment out of school. He had just gotten incredibly lucky to have a Command Centurion like Phil Kosnett, so engaged in training his officers.

Just look at Heather Lau and Siobhan Skokomish. One of these days, it would be his turn.

"Huh," Evan finally said, as Phil's words broke through the barriers that had been keeping Evan running in circles. "Think it will work?"

"I have no idea, Evan," he said, rising again and making his way to the hatch. "You eliminate most of the hay pile, and then find me any needles that remain."

"Can do, Phil," Evan said.

He looked at the screen as the hatch closed behind Phil, and started ruthlessly chopping huge chunks of data away. This would make it much faster.

Why hadn't he thought of this two days ago?

SPOILS OF WAR (SEPTEMBER 10, 402)

HEATHER SAT in the tiny wardroom aboard *Packmule* and absolutely savored today's dessert. Homemade ice cream, so fresh it had been inside a cow yesterday.

"That looks positively pornographic," Andre observed as he walked into the dining space and watched her. "Nobody should enjoy eating that much."

Heather smiled at her First Officer. *CS-405* had a fantastic head cook in Julius Gephardt, but Andre was way too much a meat-and-potatoes kind of guy.

She savored her last bite of the dish. There was nowhere else to store all the food they had stolen besides this ship, so she had the most amazing larder to pick from. And Galin Tuason had built her an ice cream maker, once they got to talking about all the fresh eggs and milk they had accumulated over the last four days.

Miniscule, on the scale of *CS-405*, with over two hundred crew, but *Packmule* had exactly eleven right now:

her regular seven, plus four cowpokes. And all that food would go bad if she didn't eat it, right?

Veggie omelets for breakfast. Milk and cream and drop biscuits with every meal. She hadn't eaten this good in years.

Andre took the seat across from her table and scowled mightily. Heather considered licking the bowl clean, like a cat.

"What's up?" she asked instead.

"I am not a veterinarian," he observed drily. "However, it appears that several of our cattle are gravid."

Wow.

"How soon?" she asked, feeling a moment of panic nip at her heels.

Cows having calves on her deck was not something Heather was prepared to handle, but they were only three days out from *Lighthouse Station*.

"It was dead of winter back on *Abakn*," Andre said. "So hopefully not immediately, but I don't know diddly squat about cows, and the cowboys are hemming and hawing about stressed animals."

"Okay," she said. "So what brings you down here?"

"I would greatly appreciate it if you could stay up late and plot the next course or two," Andre said. "I know enough astrogation to agree with the nav computer when it spits out a wild-ass guess as to where it should go. You've got a way better touch, and I'd like to get there as soon as we can, so Bok and Avelina have to deal with any calves instead of me."

Heather nodded, trying to look glum. One last,

forlorn glance at her plate of now-departed ice cream. The sooner they could get home, the better. And then she'd have to go back to just raiding the two-hundred-plus food containers for dinner.

Oh, the sacrifices we make in service.

TRUCK DRIVER (SEPTEMBER 14, 402)

IT HAD BEEN seven years since he sat in a cockpit to fly a ship. Granville told his hands to stop shaking as he walked around the shuttle, even the nearly-invisible amount they were, and focused on completing the pre-flight checklist, letting the steps calm him.

The items here were different from his old Starfighter, but he was also flying a cargo shuttle and not an armed mosquito. But the physics and technology weren't that different. He had spent the last week on a crash course to recertify as a pilot, even on the stolen freighter known as *Packmule*.

It would give him *options*.

Going home was always an option. If he wanted to face possible arrest and guaranteed humiliation as a sexual deviant. There was a new Emperor, the youngest daughter of the Emperor Granville remembered, and members of this crew had even met her when she served with this squadron as an officer. He wasn't sure it would help.

Granville still could not fathom a future where an *Emperor of Fribourg* had worn the uniform of the *Republic of Aquitaine* Navy. And yet, he was perilously close to doing the same thing.

Granville shook his head and popped open a panel on the port, rear quarter of the second insertion shuttle, the one named *Caravan*. Power at nominal levels. Fuel nearly full. Stability readings green. He closed the panel and moved around to the rear of the craft, ducking under the massive cargo container he only imagined was mooing at him.

"All good?" a voice intruded. Female.

It was still disconcerting, hearing a woman's voice on a warship deck, but he wasn't in *Fribourg* any more. Might never be, again.

He could be free. If he wanted it hard enough.

Granville turned and pulled his shoulders back just a touch. It was unconscious reflex when dealing with a superior officer. Even a woman like Captain Lau, the breveted Senior Centurion First Officer under Phil Kosnett.

He found his voice after a moment. Too much introspection.

When he was a younger son, Granville had learned to listen well before speaking. As a junior officer, the lesson had been reinforced. As a slave, pounded ruthlessly home.

Want to run away into the wilderness? Don't take a horse, or we will hunt you down and kill you. Otherwise, enjoy starving. Or being eaten by wild animals.

"All is well, Captain," Granville finally managed to bring his attention out of the past.

There was an entire future possible, right in front of him, for he and Deni.

If he had the courage to grasp it.

"You don't seem convinced," she noted dryly.

Granville suppressed a sigh. Ground his teeth a little. Chewed on the words.

"Seven years seems like yesterday, sir," he let the words escape their confinement in his soul. "And a lifetime ago, for someone I don't remember ever being."

"Understood, Veitengruber," she replied. "A week ago, you were a slave. Now, you're a pirate. I will continue to ask you what it is you want from your future. Nothing is cast in bronze right now. For you and Deni, it might never be. You have already paid us back for the effort, just by being there to rescue. If you wish to remain behind on *Lighthouse Station* and work as a hand, that is also an acceptable answer."

Granville shook his head hard. Fierce.

No, that was not it.

"I wish to pay *The Eldest* back, sir," he growled, suddenly finding the fire that had eluded him for so long. Was revenge the thing he sought most? Interesting, for such a cerebral child. "I want to join your war effort. Today, that means flying a cargo shuttle filled with cattle. Hopefully, tomorrow something more useful to the war effort."

She fixed him with a stare that apparently all command officers learned at some point. Penetrating. Almost scary, which was doubly-so coming from a woman officer, another thing his brain kept having trouble processing.

"Driving a cattle truck is at least as important as carrying a gun, Veitengruber," she snapped. "One man with a gun is dangerous. The man responsible for the cattle feeds the entire crew, and makes our war possible. Plus, you've shown us how to find more prisoners, so eventually we'll have enough crew to take something by force. *The Eldest* will learn to fear us."

Granville felt his heels snap together unconsciously. Head back. Spine ramrod straight.

For a woman officer.

But it also liberated him. He had served as a slave to the woman in charge of the cattle station. Served with men and women equally for years, overcoming his own chauvinism to become a good ranch hand. He could do this.

"Yes, sir," he replied, tight with fierce emotion.

And he had found Deni on *Abakn*. Found his other half.

Found his future under a foreign flag. Now he just had to grab hold and never let go.

"All good, Sailor?" she asked a moment later.

"Yes, sir," Granville smiled.

"Good," she smiled at him. "Don't tarry long on the surface. Just drop your boxes and pop back to orbit. Phil's called a war council for tomorrow, and I need you and Yamaguchi there with me."

"On it," he said.

She turned and strode off. Granville watched her go with something like pride growing in him. Understanding finally struck him as he moved to the rear landing skids and continued back down his checklist.

He had come home.

GHOST (SEPTEMBER 15, 402)

THE ROOM WAS CROWDED TODAY, as Heather looked around. Barely enough seats in *CS-405*'s conference room for everyone to fit. If they hadn't needed the projector, it might have been more fun to do this down on the surface of the planet around a campfire.

Evan rose at Phil's nod and moved around to the end where everyone could see him.

"The hardest part," he began suddenly, in a voice that sounded angry at himself more than anything else, "was finding a planet that doesn't exist."

That got a round of confused murmurs. Heather was already expecting something grand as an opening gambit from the Science Officer. He was like that.

"Based on interviews with Lan and Kiel, I was able to estimate a fairly small volume into which the *Mansi* system most likely existed," he continued as the voices died down. "Plus, Phil had me looking for stellar graveyards, cemeteries where old ships would be put in orbit and left, for whatever reason. There are surprisingly few of them."

Heather glanced over at Siobhan and got a nod in return. It was going to be another caper kind of operation, they both suspected.

Good thing there were a bunch of crazy pirates around here.

"However," Evan continued. "One of my target stars also had a navigation hazard listed. A *"No Go"* zone, if you will. The system itself is marked uninhabited, so it makes absolutely no sense to have that sort of marking. Except that planet is on my charts, *CS-405*'s databanks, as one that was terraformed in the ancient times."

"*Mansi?*" Heather spoke up.

"Circumstantially, but yes, sir," he nodded. "The first place we should sneak in and look around. There are no military forces listed for the system, which doesn't mean anything, since the records we stole were civilian, but even those listed stations, armed and otherwise. This is blank."

"How would you build a prison world?" Phil asked the group. "That's the question we must face. According to Lan, there is a kremlin on the surface. That's a very old, Russian word that means *fortress*. Prisoners are marched out the front gate and told to work the soil or starve. Armed stations sit in orbit, as do supposedly several captured Imperial warships. Evan?"

"Yes, sir," the Science Officer continued. "However, the records show nothing of the planet I think might be our target. There are two navigation hazards listed: one in orbit of the second planet and the second hazard being on the surface of a moon, one of fourteen orbiting a gas giant farther out. Something roughly like *Jupiter* was, back in the Home System."

"The surface of a moon?" Siobhan spoke up.

She had the only ship capable of landing on a moon. Well, Heather had three insertion shuttles, any of which could carry nearly as much cargo as *Anna* could, plus having the big containers to stow things, and the slider cranes to pick up the massive boxes.

Could they sneak *Packmule* into orbit of a messy local system like that? Without being seen? And do it on the first try?

Let's find out.

"Correct, Siobhan," Evan was saying. "The surface and not in orbit. I'm guessing that the ships in orbit of *Mansi* would be corvettes or destroyers. Maybe up to light cruisers. A Megaladon or Nightmaster could carry something like that, similar to how *Saddlebags* carries her two containers, or our cargo tug back at base hauls pods."

"So what would you put on the surface of a moon?" Heather asked.

Beside her, Granville Veitengruber tensed suddenly, as the implications struck him. Something small enough to land and take off again afterwards?

She glanced over at his quietly-nervous face and smiled encouragingly, but he kept his thoughts to himself for now.

"We'll find out when we sneak in," Phil said.

He fixed both her and Siobhan with a mean smile before he continued.

"And *CS-405* gets to do this mission," he grinned. "Neither of you have the guns or sensors to pull it off."

"Permission to come along?" Heather asked in a light-yet-formal voice.

"You and both your pilots," Phil replied. "Plus Galin Tuason. Siobhan, you'll park *Anna* out where *Packmule* hides, shut her down, and bring your entire crew over. If this works, you'll be Heather's ground team, but *Packmule* will be in orbit with us later, so we can steal as much equipment as we can get into boxes."

Phil turned to the man seated next to Heather and fixed him with a serious face.

"Lieutenant Veitengruber," he called out.

"Sir?"

"You're our resident expert on Imperial equipment," Phil said. "If we can steal it, I'll expect you to fly it out. Are you comfortable with that mission?"

Heather watched the emotions play over the younger man's face. Someone farther away than her would have probably missed it, but it was there in the way the eyes changed, the jaw clenched, the skin shifted.

"Sir, may I make one request?" Veitengruber answered after a few moments.

"You may," Phil sounded like he had been expecting something. The tone was neutral but not hostile.

"I would like to do this as a Flight Centurion, sir," Veitengruber said after a quick, deep breath.

"That's an *Aquitaine* rank, Veitengruber," Phil noted carefully.

Heather held her breath for both of them.

"I'm aware of that, sir," Granville plowed forward. "As Captain Lau pointed out to me, this is an *Aquitaine* effort, under the thin legalism of an Imperial flag. I wish to join properly, and become one of you. I understand that there is precedent."

Heather listened to a few nervous chuckles around her. Centurion Wiegand had indeed established a precedent, before she went on to become Karl VIII, *Emperor of Fribourg by Grace of God.*

"You might not be welcomed back home, if you did," Phil offered.

Granville surprised Heather, maybe as much as he did Phil, by smiling.

"My love for Deni already makes me unwelcome and suspect, Captain," Granville replied. "I cannot go back. But there is an entire future in front of me. Of us."

"I see," Phil nodded. "Have you spoken with Sri Abarantakratar about this?"

"I have not, Captain," the Imperial replied. "But it would bring me joy, so I hope it will do the same for him. He may even choose to join us, but I would not care to speak for his heart on the matter."

"So noted," Kosnett turned to Heather and nodded to her.

There were entire chapters of dialog in that simple nod. While Phil was in command of the squadron, Heather Lau had breveted to Command Centurion when she took over *Packmule.* The task of enlisting Granville Veitengruber, all the oaths, *everything,* was her responsibility as the man's commanding officer.

She turned to look at the man, noting that the apprehension had returned to his face. She smiled and nodded silently to put him at ease.

"You're sure?" Heather asked.

"I am," his voice suddenly got emotional.

"Welcome aboard, then," Heather smiled.

One more hand would make the job easier. Two would be even better, but she would need to approach Deni privately.

He had kept mostly to himself since the rescue, sharing a room with Granville and joining them for meals, or when strong backs were needed, but he largely stayed in the cabin and studied histories of the Empire and the Republic.

Another one, like Granville, that might never go home.

"Any other questions?" Phil looked around the group. "We don't know much yet, but everyone should plan for a mission to sneak into a system, like we did *Laptev*, followed by planetary insertion, then a case of grand theft starship. Nothing? Dismissed."

Heather made her way aft with many of the rest. The flight deck on *CS-405* was just barely big enough for the one admin shuttle, *Cherokee*, so she would catch a ride back to bring Andre up to speed. After that, a promotion ceremony to plan.

And then, who knew what craziness would come?

COWBOY (SEPTEMBER 20, 402)

BOK PULLED the reins on the roan mare and pointed her head back up the slope, instead of down towards the lake like she wanted to go. They were still coming to an understanding about things, but he was more stubborn than the horse.

Than any horse.

Three small herds of cattle stretched out around him as he rode. Heather had brought just over one hundred and fifty head, and he had four big pastures fenced off for them to graze.

They were mostly settling in. Better than the horses, anyway. Helped that cattle weren't as smart, and really didn't care, as long as they had grass to feed on and the weather wasn't too ugly. And as near as Bok could tell, his half of the valley was never going to get all that cold, at least compared to where they had just come from.

Sounds of another horse brought his head around. Able Spacer Epifania Gaufusi, *Effie*, riding the young, black stallion like she had been born in the saddle. She might have. Bok hadn't pressed too closely into the background of his volunteers for this bizarre colony called *Lighthouse Station.*

And it was just the four of them now: him, Avelina, Epifania, and Shelby, at least until someone came back for them. Or *Buran* discovered the place. Just one ranch in the middle of nowhere. Kinda like he had once dreamed of retiring to.

"What's the word?" Bok asked as she reined in next to him. The big black she had named *Avalanche*, on account of how he ran. The roan hadn't rated a name yet. She was still too fussy.

"Sensors have been picking up a creature at night," Effie said. "Close to the fence, but hasn't worked up the gumption to cross, with the lights suddenly flashing in its eyes. Rode over and found some signs."

"What is it?" Bok asked, reaching back on his saddle to touch the pulse rifle and confirm he had packed it this morning.

Jessica Keller had once invaded an Imperial planet with a legion of crazy rednecks on horses, but Bok was just a cowboy at heart. Grew up with the lariat and the rifle. Not much had changed in fifty years.

"Medium sized cat," Effie replied. "Closest system match I could find was something called a Jaguarondi."

"Huh," Bok observed. "Show me."

Effie kneed Avalanche into motion and Bok let the roan follow, only touching the reins when the horse wanted to skitter along and start racing the black. Bok figured the roan was about five years old, but Avalanche was just past being a colt, so he would be a pretty good stud when time came.

If they ended up colonizing this rock for the rest of their lives, for instance.

Effie led him to a gate that the crew had built in when they'd added all the wires, sensors, and strobe lights to scare off cats. Outside the fence, a trail ran all the way around the property. Bok checked that his comm was on, but he could see the farmhouse and the stack of containers from here, just about a kilometer distant, not far from the shore of the lake on a nice promontory that stuck a little ways out into the water.

Effie headed clockwise, towards the higher end of the lake.

The whole valley was a self-contained watershed and ecosystem. Birds could get in, but larger creatures had to really want to cross one of the high passes, and none of those routes were soft or pleasant. The high end of the valley butted up against the grandfather of all the other mountains that formed the bowl around here, a long-extinct stratovolcano that had long ago kicked out all sorts of stuff to make the valley below so fertile.

If the weather was likely to get a little better in the summer, Bok would have eventually wanted to plant grapes. He added that to the list of plants he needed to find. With ten thousand years, something grape-like might have evolved to local conditions. The trees were strange enough variants of things he knew from back home, maybe evolved originally from Douglas-fir or sequoia, but they cut and burned just fine.

Effie pulled Avalanche up short and dismounted. Bok

stayed a-horseback and drew the pulse rifle from the saddle holster. Canine species might hunt, but tended to run away when confronted with bigger creatures they didn't know.

Cats, on the other hand, would hunt you if they thought they could get away with it. Jaguarondi might be a small puma, according to the records he remembered. Dark and sleek, but not a full-sized beast, if he was lucky. Not a threat to a group of cattle that would kick and stomp, but the new calves he was expecting would be at risk.

And he wasn't about to allow wild cats anywhere near the station. If the cost was being overrun with rats and rabbits, he would just have to come up with something to poison the former and ignore the latter.

Rabbits made a wonderful alarm. If you had them around, there were no medium- to large-sized predators running around. Bok hadn't seen birds big enough to be a threat to humans or calves.

He could always jury-rig an air-defense turret with a stun cannon if he needed to chase eagles off.

"Here," Effie said, pointing to a spot on the ground.

To clear pasture for fencing, and get enough wood for everything they needed to build, the crew had opened a corridor forty meters wide. There were still patches of trees inside the fence, but part of the reason Bok had chosen this spot was the series of connected meadows, probably cleared by regular wildfires caused by lightning.

In the future, cattle and humans would alter the local biosystems instead.

Effie realized Bok was holding a rifle, so she pulled a pulse pistol from her hip as she looked at him.

"Problem?" she asked carefully.

"Jaguarondi's probably too small to attack us," Bok noted. "Don't know if we've gotten into his range with fence-building, or he's decided to move into ours. Don't plan on being a friendly neighbor about it."

Bok turned the roan's head uphill and pushed her into motion. Effie mounted a moment later and joined them.

It wasn't tropical jungle up here, so the going wasn't that rough. Overhead, a green canopy that was about an even mix of deciduous and evergreen. A lot of what he wanted to call Douglas fir mixed in with oaks and maples, if he understood the leaf patterns.

There was a stand of sequoia not far from here that Bok planned to leave alone. At least seventy-five of the ancient monsters reaching for the sky, at least by their size today.

Bok knew there were enough deer and such that game trails would exist. Didn't take long to find one and inspect it.

"Eyes up, just in case," he said as he dismounted, rifle still in hand.

Bok figured that the roan would spook if she smelled a cat getting close, but it might be sitting in the trees. There were a few with branches low enough and big enough that a cat could hide in them.

And the cat had come through here at some point. Bok found a partial print that was too big to be a housecat, and too small to be a lion. About the size of a dog, maybe.

Just the one print, and going away. Cat had stepped in a puddle, so maybe at a dead run. And sure as hell wasn't going to wait around for Bok to track him.

Bok sighed and mounted up. This time he let the roan head downhill, as was her preference, and nodded Effie into motion.

"We'll have to modify the sensors," he thought aloud. "And probably bait a trap with some fresh kill. First, we'll need to build a turret that we can control from the farmhouse."

"Stunner?" Effie asked.

"Negative," Bok decided. "Any predator that comes down to the wire after carrion gets killed. If we end up wiping out all the things keeping the deer in check, we'll just have to start farming them, too."

"Venison's good meat," she noted.

Bok nodded. This was his valley. His planet, at least until Avelina carried through with her threat to claim the entire place as an Imperial world and get herself made Duke of it.

Or *Buran* showed up to challenge his claim.

RAIDER (SEPTEMBER 29, 402)

PHIL CAUGHT himself referring to the group today as the varsity squad. That suggested that the team he had been using were junior varsity. It was possibly accurate, but still rather insulting. They had done a fantastic job, growing into new responsibilities as he stretched this small crew thinner and thinner.

But today, he had everyone back. Heather in her normal slot forward on the Emergency Bridge. Siobhan piloting here on the bridge and bickering good-naturedly with Evan in the Science Officer station again.

The only person really missing was Bok Battenhouse, the Boatswain, but Kam was still a better engineer, plus Galin and Markus were aboard today, watching everything and taking notes.

He hadn't even had to order Siobhan and Heather back into uniform. Both had gotten up today and returned to active service. Or they were playing roles, and tomorrow would go back to being pirates. He figured the latter was more likely, but wasn't going to push.

Next year, they were going to probably have issues, when the *RAN* required them to act like grown-ups again.

"Sixty seconds to *Emergence*," Siobhan called on all channels.

"Sciences?" Phil said aloud.

"Fore and Aft systems both active and ready for passive scan, Commander," Evan replied.

"Engineering?" Phil continued.

"Secondary JumpSails are holding well enough," Kam replied. "We'll be able to run if we have to."

Good. This had been a very short jump, exactly for that reason. A full day spent out at the inner edge of the Oort Cloud, just listening to every electronic chirp and looking for planets and other objects moving.

At *Trusski*, *RAN Ballard* had gotten the glory by forward-spotting from the shadows of a moon. At *Laptev*, Phil's crew had proven themselves just as good.

Here, it was likely to be even more hairy.

If this truly was *Mansi*, and they only had a pretty good, gut feeling still, the locals were likely to be much more paranoid. Doubly so if anyone had come through lately and warned them of pirates loose in the *Altai* sector or shared tales of Jessica Keller's devastating raids along the inner part of the frontier, along this side of *M'Hanii*.

But paranoia bred stress, and that was a significant chunk of his purpose. Keller would have had to withdraw, having lost *CS-405* without explanation after *Severnaya Zemlya*. She would need time to move the Forward Base to a new hiding place. Time that would have let *Buran* recover some of his footing.

Hopefully that deathless bastard was pouring resources into the *Altai* sector to look for Phil's pirates. Not enough to actually find him, but enough that they had to come from somewhere else, meaning Keller might stumble into an unguarded system with a warpack set to fight a major fleet action.

Goths finding an unlocked, postern gate.

Phil just wished there was a way to easily get her a message. Right now, that would involve a sixty-day sail back to *Osynth B'Udan*, just to find someone who could direct him back to the front lines with *Mendocino* or *Duncan*.

"All hands, stand by," Siobhan said in her best radio voice. "*Emergence.*"

Phil felt it in his bones today, but just watching the stress suddenly rise in Siobhan and Evan's backs told him they had arrived. He gave them thirty seconds to absorb everything before he spoke.

"Evan. Status?" Phil asked in a command voice. He still had the interior lines open, so everyone was listening. Not standard procedure, but today it felt appropriate.

"Well in the shadow of moon *Three*," Evan said.

The gas giant behind them was tentatively listed as *Mansi-D*, assuming this was the right system. Its moons were numbered down from largest to smallest. Number *One* was volcanic, spewing the occasional lava plume into orbit, as it was too close to the primary for comfort and got squished constantly by moving gravity fields on all sides. *Two* was an icemoon much further away from the gas giant, with the possibility of a major, liquid ocean underneath, depending on how one interpreted the data.

Three was a rock. Pretty big as moons went, perhaps thirty-five hundred kilometers in diameter. It was tidally locked with the primary, always presenting the same face inward, with what looked like a thin-but-measurable atmosphere mostly made up of nitrogen and carbon dioxide, from what Evan was forwarding to his station.

"Siobhan?" Phil asked.

"Dead center on target zone and holding," his Pilot replied, still sounding too much like *Lady Blackbeard* for this deck.

CS-405 was between *Three* and *D*. Hiding from any sensors over on *Mansi-B*, itself down on the warmer, inner edge of this system's habitable zone. The ship would slowly orbit in retrograde to the moon below them, hiding behind the rock as it orbited the primary. A full orbit would take about three days, but they weren't going to be here that long.

"Maintain shadow holding," Phil ordered. "Evan, anything below us on the ground looking up?"

"Negative," the Science Officer said after a tense moment. "I can see beacons on the surface, and a few in orbit above us, but they appear to be navigational in nature, sir. All are emitting a matching signal, so I would guess you could use them to triangulate your location in three dimensions with reasonable accuracy. Nobody is painting us with a sensor that I can detect."

"Assume passives and mark them for destruction on a later pass, as necessary," Phil said.

If he could sneak in and out a few more times, that

would be lovely, but blowing things up remained high on his list, because anything he killed had to be replaced by that stupid robot.

It wasn't a butterfly's wings causing a hurricane, but every bit of entropy he could deliver was one less that Keller had to, or opened the door for her and *Fribourg* one millimeter farther.

Phil listened for five, tense minutes as all hands went about their business. He kept quiet and let the experts handle things at this point. Everybody had been briefed on the needs from their stations, and they were among the very best, or they wouldn't be here in the first place.

Finally, the little clock on his screen ticked down to zero. Time for higher-risk adventure to start.

"Pilot, stand by to broach," Phil ordered in his big, serious voice. "Science Officer, you have Tactical."

Normally, Heather was the Tactical officer, but today she was just Second in Command. Evan Brinich would have control of things as he needed for the most delicate task ahead.

"Pilot," Evan called, never looking up from his boards. "Prepare to bring our tail around a little more, roughly eight degrees as we climb out."

"Roger that," Siobhan replied seriously, all merriment and teasing from their two voices gone.

Phil hadn't seen a Hammerhead over there in their earlier scans, but he had no idea what a secret prison on a hidden planet might have for defenses. And there was only so much you could see from thirty light-hours away.

"Execute your broach," Evan commanded.

On Phil's screens, *CS-405* edged below the south pole

of *Three* and was suddenly inundated by a mass of signals traffic from *Mansi-B*, the prison world.

They were behind *Mansi-B* in orbit, with that world moving farther away from them every day. About a quarter orbit separated them right now, so the signals were a little stale, but not much. Less than an hour old.

No active ships in orbit.

Not just no warships, but no ships of any kind. Nothing at all here, with the other navigational hazard well away from the planet. Just eight stations defining a perfect cube, at forty-five north and forty-five south latitude, geosynchronous with the ground, ninety degrees apart. Phil doubted that Evan would be able to spot the kremlin on the ground from here, but he didn't need to know where it was. There was nothing his force could do against a heavily-defended planet, and those eight stations were each big enough that they probably had serious firepower aboard them.

But at the same time, they couldn't move. There were no ships visible that could come over here if they did spot him. That either meant they were on the planetary surface, where *The Eldest* would never have left them, being too valuable, or they were so small that they could dock inside one of the stations.

Anything that tiny he could splatter with *CS-405*'s pulse beams if they got too close.

All that meant was that Phil only had to worry about external visitors, coming on some schedule he could not predict.

A freighter full of new prisoners he might be able to intercept, if he was in exactly the perfect position at the right moment, which he doubted. Alternatively, he would be facing something too big to challenge, from a single Hammerhead all the way up to a Megalodon carrying a newly captured cruiser to deposit in orbit over there.

No, if this was really *Mansi*, as Lan had described the place, all Phil and his people could do would be to confirm it, and then run like hell for home without the locals knowing they had been scouted. *Fribourg* would need to bring a fleet big enough to take the system and hold it long enough to locate and evacuate all Imperial prisoners.

Idly, Phil wondered if that sort of thing might get him knighted, like Arlo and Kermode had been. He was still facing the possibility of a hostile Court Martial at *Ladaux*, for having his primary JumpSail destroyed and the secondary so badly mangled while escaping that they were required to limp along even slower than *Queen Anne's Revenge* or *Packmule*.

Anything he could do to balance that ledger out a little before he went home to his fate would be worth doing.

"Pilot, secure from broach," Evan called, breaking Phil out of his reverie and bringing him back to the present.

He hadn't been daydreaming, so much as planning the next six stages of his campaign. Too much hinged on the data Evan had gathered today, and how soon it could be turned into information.

Around them, *CS-405* slid silently back below the horizon of *Three*, as seen from *Mansi-B*.

"Stand by for a hard ping on the ground," Evan said.

This had to wait until last. They might trigger something on the ground by scanning everything. And the reflection might bounce enough energy off the surface of *Mansi-D* that someone paying attention might see something and grow curious.

CS-405 needed to be long gone before anyone came to investigate.

"Executing," Evan called loudly to the room and the whole ship.

Two hard pulses of energy, aimed straight down, covering an area around three thousand kilometers across, so hopefully none of the energy bled around the horizon to be picked up closer to the inhabited parts of the system.

"Secured from scanning," Evan pressed a button on his board and leaned back a little. "Pilot, take us into Jump."

Siobhan pressed *405* sideways into JumpSpace before Evan had finished speaking, the tiny escort leaping away for the safe depths of interstellar space.

"Commander, you have the bridge," Evan said formally. "Ship is in JumpSpace."

"All hands, secure from General Quarters," Phil replied. "Stand down and return to normal crew rotations."

Meaning, Phil was back down to the junior varsity team, which was getting to be good enough that they might give the main players a run for it, given a few more months of being First Violinists. But Heather and Siobhan could turn over their stations and get some food and a nap.

They would need to be ready for the next phase of planning.

BANDITS (OCTOBER 1, 402)

HEATHER HAD BLOWN up a map of the third moon and printed it on a meter-square piece of paper, where it hung on the wall of *Packmule's* bridge as a reminder of what to look forward to, as she killed time on her watch, until Andre woke up.

The timing of the scouting run had been random luck, but it hadn't worked out too bad. The surface of the moon was a battered pizza dough where bubbles had popped while cooking, leaving a few hills, a number of weirdly-flat craters, and several rocky seas made up of what Evan had guessed were volcanic plains left over from planetary formation. They hadn't noted any active volcanoes during their pass, but there had to be something, since the atmosphere, however thin it was, was being actively replenished faster than the gas giant overhead could strip molecules away.

Evan had noted three places where they might find

things on the surface, but one of them had been right at the terminator of his scan, so there might be more beyond it.

What was there was interesting enough to warrant a raid.

Unlike *Aquitaine*, *Fribourg* maintained a rigid ship scaling system. A-type were individually-piloted star fighters, while B-type were multi-crew bombers and gunships, still operating from a mothership carrier. They were both easily distinguished from larger vessels by lacking any jump capabilities.

The surface showed what looked like old Imperial fighters, including a few of the *A-7b* fighters and the venerable *A-3f* strike fighters. Veitengruber had been flying an *A-6j* fighter seven years ago when he was captured at *Samara*.

At one of the target zones, Evan had flagged what looked like a line of old C-type Cutters, normally used for Search & Rescue and Customs Enforcement. Police more than military. Why and how *Buran* had captured them suggested raids on other systems that *Fribourg* hadn't talked too much about.

At the other primary zone, Evan had flagged what looked like a pair of D-type escorts, which were far more common in *Fribourg* service, usually permanently attached to big carrier squadrons as the outermost ring of defenses.

Heather was torn as she stared at the image. She had reviewed the recognition files on both types of boats. D-type ships were bigger by about a third, on average, and better armed, with a pair of Type-2 beams, a pair of Type-1's, and two missile tubes.

They were still eggshells with guns, against anything that could shoot back, including snubfighters.

C-type hulls, the police cutters, tended to have a single, bigger Type-3 beam on the bow with a good arc, and a pair of Type-1's with side coverage. As ships, they weren't much bigger than *Queen Anne's Revenge*, when you got right down to it, with a big gun wrapped by tissue paper shields.

Still, if they managed to steal one, it would immediately become the second-most dangerous vessel in the squadron, just for having guns. Even if Phil stripped some for *CS-405*.

Heather called up a roster and checked the time. Galin was awake. She would ask the engineer his thoughts. This would be her raid, Phil had been clear, since she was the only one who could remove significant parts from the surface. *Anna* had tools and a repulsor truck with a winch, but very little internal space for something at this scale. Heather had a number of empty storage containers now, with so much food transferred to the other vessels.

"Tuason," the man replied when the line opened.

"You studied enough Imperial engineering to dismantle ships on the ground?" Heather asked.

"Maybe," the engineer said after a beat. "What were you wanting to steal?"

"Guns off of a carcass on the ground, with minimal time, rednecked tools, and trouble overhead," Heather said, grinning at the usual impossible deadlines in Navy service.

"Wouldn't it be easier to fly them off to zero-g and

strip them there?" he asked, getting exactly to the center of her conundrum.

Nobody had any idea what kind of shutdown procedure *Buran* had done when they put the ships on the ground. It hadn't been freefall from orbit. Maybe a larger ship or a tug had dropped them like cargo containers, but many were in solid shape, at least from the pictures.

She and the pirates would have to walk aboard and push buttons. Hopefully, there was enough fuel for reactors and engines to lift off. The surface gravity would only be about one-seventh, so they didn't need much, but they would have to transition to JumpSpace to truly get away.

Packmule wasn't a carrier that could launch a bunch of fighters. And they didn't have the manpower or equipment to convert enough of the ships to pull it off, even after she had asked Galin and Markus for a few ideas. They had come back with something like a *Corynthe* Mothership, with random small craft docked ass-inward into a silo made from four shipping containers.

"You and Markus will be on the ground with Kam," she said, invoking *CS-405*'s Chief Engineer, Kamila Rushforth. "Granville will be there as well, but he's going to focus on ships. I want you thinking about getting us guns. Anything to alter the balance of power on a raid."

"Gotcha, boss," Galin said.

She cut the line and went back to enjoying a good funk. There were no right answers here. Probably no wrong ones, either, with everything on a long, fine grade of grays.

What was the best way to skin that cat?

A second thought struck her and she keyed the man's cabin. System showed Veitengruber was awake. Probably reading, since lights were on and the video system playing.

They weren't on a formal watch rotation right now. Not with only nine crew.

"This is Veitengruber," the voice came back a second later.

"Granville, it's Heather," she replied. "I'd like to spend a few minutes with you on the bridge, going over things while I have some questions."

It sounded like a request, but it really wasn't. She was Command Centurion here. And in command of the raiding teams.

"Be right there, sir," the man said.

The line went dead a beat later and Heather was alone with her thoughts. The team on the ground was going to be alone for at least two and a half days, observing radio silence, assuming everything went well. Enough time to get into trouble. Not enough to get out.

They would be running down the thin edge of the blade on this one.

The hatch slid open and the Imperial appeared.

Ex-Imperial. Granville Veitengruber wore the black and green of an *Aquitaine* Centurion today, with Flight tags for now, although she had suggested that he was probably too old to requalify in snubfighters, once they got home, and would need to pick a new career track.

He had asked if they had a tag for piracy. Fortunately, neither Phil nor Siobhan were around at the time, or they might have taken the man seriously. With all that that might have entailed.

"Sit," she pointed, before he could come to attention and salute, or any of that.

The man took the pilot's chair with a curious face.

Heather went back to studying the map on the wall.

"We won't have time to steal everything I want to from the surface of *Three*," she began.

Granville nodded. That much was self-evident, for the pirates.

"What are your thoughts on prioritization, Centurion?" she continued.

She watched his face relax as his thoughts wandered inward.

"My personal preference would be a Starfighter for myself," he said with a grin they shared. "But since that's not an option, I lean towards a C-boat. The D-class has better armaments, but we would need a crew of at least twenty to work it effectively, and I don't see where we could recruit them, short of going home and falling under Formal Order again."

Formal Order. The rules and regulations that made up the *Fribourg* Fleet. An end to piracy, as it were.

"It would be nice to steal some missiles off of a D-carcass, if we could," Granville mused. "I bet we've got enough crazy engineers to mount them in the belly of *Queen Anne's Revenge* as a Q-ship. Or rebuild a pair of cargo containers as missile racks. Fly one of the shuttles right up to a station and then hammer the shit out it when their shields are down."

"You willing to fly that mission, Centurion?" she asked, voice suddenly serious.

Something caught his ear. He turned to her and she could see seven years of forced servitude, slavery, well up inside with a red tinge of anger.

"Aye, sir," he growled.

She nodded and keyed a comm switch.

"Tuason," Galin acknowledged.

"You doing anything in engineering that you can't leave, or watch from up here?" Heather asked.

"Negative," the man said. "Be right there."

"Forlorn mission?" Granville asked.

It was a formal term, for sailors. Technically not a suicide mission, since there was always a chance you could do whatever job you had in front of you, and still escape afterward. It was still a slim chance, usually. Either a full frontal assault against overwhelming defenders, just to distract them, or a last-ditch defense, *Horatio holding the bridge by himself* sort of thing.

"I don't think so," Heather snapped back sarcastically. "Pirates don't go all in for that death or glory thing, Sailor. We're here to steal shit and make a profit in the process."

"I see," he relaxed again as she watched. "And armed stations over prison planets?"

"A bank vault that needs to be bypassed," she grinned. "Blowing the damned thing in place is always an option, since we are not going to have the right cover story to sneak in. And we only have to take out one of them, as near as I can tell. The other seven might fire missiles at us, but that's about all they can do, and *CS-405* is an escort specifically designed for things like that."

"What's up, boss?" Galin said as he came through the hatch.

Heather pointed at the poster as an introduction.

"How many standard, Imperial missiles could you fit into a single shipping container, if you wanted to fire them with surprise at a short-range target?" she asked, gesturing at Granville.

"Three for sure," he replied instantly. "Had this talk with Markus and Bok at one point. Technically, you could fit six in there, fired in two salvos of three, but you need to have a blast barrier mid-way down to protect the back three. Then you have to come up with a way to clear it as a blockage before firing the second batch."

"What about hinged pie-slices?" Granville suddenly asked. "Attached to the outer skin so they can retract upward and open the throat, once the first batch is clear?"

"Take about ten or fifteen seconds," Galin guessed. "Pretty good chance that at least one of that second batch fails from heat and pressure and then either explodes in the tube, or turns sideways and maybe flies through the shuttle."

"I can live with those odds, Galin," Granville spoke up before Heather could reply.

"Boss?" Galin turned to her.

"Draw me up plans," Heather decided. "We won't know until we land what we can steal, but that adds one hell of a safe-cracker to the mix. How about fuel?"

"We've got enough to keep flying for maybe decade," Galin smiled. "Easy enough to top off one of the shipping containers and send it down with *Caravan* or *Saddlebags*.

Even empty, we ought to be able to get more things to orbit than we can fly."

"Today, Galin," she corrected him.

"Sir?"

"More things than we can fly with the two hundred people we have on hand *today*," she continued. "There's a whole planet of folks we can recruit, once we can kick the front door in."

WAR PLAN (OCTOBER 3, 402)

Siobhan practically salivated at the possibilities as *405*'s shuttle docked with *Packmule* to pick up the rest of the crazies. Right up until she did the math and realized that it was a losing proposition.

On the one hand, stealing a pocket warship from the little moon would give them something that they could get dangerous with. But they were running dangerously thin on crew right now. And Phil wasn't about to send Lan and Kiel on their merry ways with *Queen Anne's Revenge*. Their ship was still the best way to sneak into an unsuspecting port, at least until *Buran* figured that trick out, which Siobhan didn't expect to happen anytime soon.

Those folks tended to be even more linear than Imperials, if that was possible.

The shuttle thumped and clanged as the airlocks mated. It was easy enough to do it this way, rather than rearranging the small flight deck on *Packmule* to land a shuttle. The airlock beeped its way open and people began joining them.

Galin and Veitengruber looked too proud of themselves. Yamaguchi had a goofy grin. Well, goofier than usual. Andre looked like he had sucked a lemon, but that was normal for him.

When Heather boarded last, Siobhan knew there was something utterly evil afoot. The woman practically glowed as she slid into the seat next to Siobhan and grinned.

"Out with it," *Lady Blackbeard* growled. "You're up to no good. And doing it without me."

"Perish the thought," Heather replied snidely. "You'll be there with us. Promise."

"Uh huh," Siobhan was not mollified.

"Besides," Heather continued in a voice made of honey. "I don't want to have to explain it twice, and Phil still needs to give his blessing."

"Worse than anything we've done so far?" Siobhan caught her breath.

They had raided mining colonies and stolen trucks, freighters, cattle, horses, chickens, and one sixth of the sector's food transport network. What would top that?

Siobhan felt a growing excitement, just at the possibilities, but the others remained aloof for the rest of the flight over. Grinning silently to any question she or Trinidad or Markus put to them, eyes big and bright and innocent.

Like she was going to believe any of that.

It felt like forever before they finally docked with *CS-405*. Interminable trudging through hallways to get to the conference room that seemed to be where all the best plans got hatched.

Phil was already there, along with Kam and Evan. The dozen people with Siobhan filled the space to capacity.

Phil looked at her, and then Heather. Siobhan figured the man was suppressing an eyeroll as everyone settled.

"Andre," Phil began. "You look the most sour, especially compared to Heather. What terrible news did she share with you?"

Siobhan nearly giggled at the side-eye from the nurse who was 2IC on *Packmule* now.

"That I'll be in charge for several days," Andre said. "While those people are off having adventures on the surface of *Three*."

"Really?" Phil asked with a grin. "So you'd have bridge time under your belt, if I needed to put Evan on an independent command and pull you back aboard *405* as my temporary First Officer?"

The room erupted into howls of laughter at the terrible, thunderous scowl that overcame Andre's face. Any time he had to leave Medbay, for any reason, Andre grumbled. Not much. He was an officer and took his job seriously, but would have happily spent his entire career at a base hospital somewhere.

"Why can't Kermit handle the job?" Andre finally grumbled, referring to *405*'s Surgeon, Senior Centurion Kermit Hanley. Another one like Andre, who would have happily remained in Medical, handing out aspirin and taking temperatures of sailors with sniffles.

"Oh, I'd send him over to *Packmule* to replace you," Phil smiled. "Have Heather get him bridge time as well.

Need to have trained medical staff on as many ships as we can."

That suddenly brought an evil, wicked smile to Andre's face. Perhaps enough to actually consider doing it, if he could give his own boss, his former boss, whatever, the same sort of discomfort that came from making life and death decisions on the bridge, rather than the operating table.

"Okay, Heather," Phil grinned and turned to the two primary pirates, Heather sitting next to Siobhan. "I've teased Andre enough and somewhere, Kermit's ears are burning. What have you got for me?"

"How do you feel about a full, frontal assault on *Mansi-B*?" Heather grinned back. Butter wouldn't melt in her mouth right now.

"Possibly the dumbest idea I've ever heard," Phil replied. "Why do you think it might work?"

Heather gestured to Galin and Veitengruber.

"Been consulting my experts," Heather said. "None of us can see any reason for *Buran* to remove missiles from captured ships, and if they did, why do more than stack them nearby for safe keeping?"

"That station will have enough defenses to stop a sortie of missiles," Phil noted, his voice growing serious.

"Not if we sail right up to it and punch him in the mouth," Heather's smile also got serious.

Siobhan's breath caught.

Audacity itself.

"Talk to me," Phil commanded.

"*Packmule* drops into system with special orders that need to be hand delivered, plus a secret cargo for the surface," Heather began. "Centurion Veitengruber flies *Caravan* over like he's going to make the delivery. As they bring their shields down, he fires twelve missiles from point blank, if everything works. Show me a station that can take that level of damage, especially if more pirates come along and rake the place with beams after he's been knocked down."

"Twelve?" Phil turned to Galin with a feral gleam in his eyes.

"Think so, Commander," the engineer stood his ground. "I can put three in a container, with another three as a second salvo behind them after the first set fires. Two containers. Six in the first salvo shouldn't be any problem. Might blow up the shuttle firing the other six."

"Odds?" Phil pressed.

Galin shrugged. Siobhan agreed. They were down to counting angels on the head of a pin at that point.

"Veitengruber?" Phil turned to his newest crew member.

"Noble tasks tend to be the most dangerous, sir," the ex-Imperial replied in a somber voice. "Is there anything more noble that rescuing all my old comrades from this fate?"

"Okay," Phil acknowledged.

Easy as that.

"Tell me the rest."

"My goal is to land *Saddlebags*, *Caravan*, and *Anna* on the surface of *Three*," Heather said. "With as many engineers and crew as you can risk being caught on the surface, if something goes wrong. Galin and Markus for sure. I'd like Kam, too, if we can, since Bok's not here and he'd be the third leg."

"Already part of the overall plan," Kam spoke up. "Someone needs to keep the pirates in line."

Another laugh rippled around the room. They were all pirates now.

"I'm aiming to get a C-class hull working, if we can, and fly it off," Heather said. "That will be Veitengruber, for now. Then we'll pivot to the D-class boats and the fighters sitting on the ground, to be stripped for parts. Any missiles we can liberate get trucked into *Anna* and the insertion shuttles."

"Why not a D-type?" Phil asked. "Why settle for a C?"

"Not enough warm bodies," Heather replied. "However, once we steal everything and go back to *Lighthouse Station*, the plan is to come back and blow apart one of *Mansi-B*'s stations, if we can, and liberate as many prisoners as can get away. That gives us enough crew to do all sorts of dangerously crazy things, all over the sector. You'll have to brevet to Imperial Admiral, by the way, Phil."

Siobhan grinned as that tidbit wormed its way into Phil's mind, lighting up his eyes in interesting ways. He obviously hadn't considered that they might build a wolfpack out here, stealing all this junk. Or have enough crew to do something with it. But they were his plans, originally. She and Heather were just seeing them to fruition.

Phil Kosnett, commander of the smallest warship in

RAN service, might become Admiral Kosnett of Second Expeditionary Fleet.

And butter still wouldn't melt in Heather's mouth right now.

Siobhan couldn't wait.

PORTALS (OCTOBER 11, 402)

It still felt weird to proudly wear the uniform that had been that of his worst enemy a decade ago. But it also felt right.

Granville knew that he would never willingly return to Imperial Service. Would never even set foot in Imperial space one minute longer than absolutely necessary to fill out paperwork forever separating him from the places he had known as a child and the family that would never accept him as an adult.

Not while he was with Deni. And that was not negotiable.

They would find a new place to exist. *Aquitaine* didn't care about his personal affairs, unless they proved detrimental to the *Good Conduct Of The Navy*. A navy that allowed women to serve as equals.

But to go to the *Republic* would take Deni a quarter of the galaxy from his home, although nobody knew if

NovLao had managed to survive the patient onslaught of *Buran*.

Deni had been a soldier, not a sailor. A squad commander roughly equivalent to a sergeant, captured during the invasion of *Douangdeuane* and shipped off to serve *The Holding* as a manual laborer on a planet so far from home that his home stars weren't even visible from here.

NovLao would not care any more than *Aquitaine* about love.

Their cabin was dim. Deni was asleep on the bed while Granville sat in a reclining chair and familiarized himself with everything the *Republic of Aquitaine* Navy knew about every variant of C- and D-type vessels that Fribourg had ever launched.

He thought he was being quiet, but Deni stirred and rolled over. Probably the light.

"Will there be a test later?" Deni asked with sly humor as he noted the tablet in Granville's hands. "Will it be necessary to strip an engine while blindfolded?"

Granville grinned. Deni was one of the few people who could pierce the barriers Granville kept about himself. Usually by puncturing the pomposity that tended to build up. Always, Imperial Officer and Gentleman, fierce and militant.

Except when he wasn't.

"There will not," Granville allowed. "They'll even allow me to take my notes with me."

"Then why are you staying up all night studying?" Deni asked.

It wasn't a question he could answer easily.

Well, it was, but that would require admitting things about himself. Which he could do, here in this cabin, with nobody but his beloved around.

"Fear," Granville said in a tiny voice.

It was perhaps the most honest answer he could give.

"Of?" Deni pressed.

"Losing you," Granville admitted finally. "I could die in battle happily. Or I could become a hero. But I don't know what comes after this war. After we get back to friendly territory."

"Having second thoughts?" Deni asked. His voice was teasing, but his eyes were serious.

"The only second thoughts I have are trying to guess where we might be happiest, Deni," Granville replied. "Do we return to *Aquitaine*? *NovLao*? Should we just stay on *Lighthouse Station* for the rest of our lives, where nobody can find us? Hell, Keller's apparently a queen of someplace called *Corynthe*, clear out on the very edge of the galaxy itself. Should we go there?"

Deni shrugged and sat up, sliding back against the wall.

"What would make you happy, Granvie?" he asked.

"You," Granville said simply. It really was as easy as that, when you cut away all the other details.

He just had to have the courage to admit that to himself.

"And do you care where we go, as long as we're together?" Deni probed.

"No."

It really was that easy. Granville smiled.

"Then you should come to bed," Deni said, sliding

over. "I'm cold and you need the sleep, if you're going to go off and be a hero tomorrow."

"You'll be with me," Granville pointed out, powering off the machine and sliding out of his shoes.

"Ah, but I'm just a strong back accustomed to taking orders, *Flight Centurion*," Deni's tease was back. "I have no inclination to become a hero."

"You're my hero," Granville said as he pulled off his tunic and slid under the warm covers.

"That just goes to show how foolish we can all be."

Granville grinned and kissed him.

Where would he be without Deni? Granville knew he would have never survived captivity long, but for this man.

Tomorrow, they might be heroes. Or dead.

But they would be together. That was the only important part.

THREE (OCTOBER 12, 402)

Heather forced herself to relax as she watched the board on the pilot's station. Andre was going to be in charge as soon as she left, so she had made him sit in the Director's chair from the moment he had come aft from his cabin.

The muttering under his breath was mostly just Andre talking to himself, rather than true grumbling. Mundane stuff like the unfairness of life, and what had he done to anger the gods.

Andre being Andre.

Siobhan had gone ahead of them on the raid in *Anna*, once *405* had confirmed that nothing appeared to have changed about the system. Still no other ships transmitting signals. Just the eight sentinels in orbit of *Mansi-B*.

The trick with doing something like this, with JumpDrives instead of sails, was to turn off every single external system that might emit a signal, including shields and sensors. And then to jump from the far edge of the system to a spot that should be behind *Mansi-D*, when seen from the surface of the prison planet.

Then pause and pray while the engines recharged and you sat with passive sensors hoping to not see anything suddenly looming out of the fog.

CS-405 had a distinct advantage here, since it could just ride the JumpSails, however primitive and underpowered the secondaries were, and drop out of space exactly where they wanted to be, without much risk of scattering.

A signal on Heather's board cut through the tension.

Siobhan had dropped into her spot in the shadow of *Three. Queen Anne's Revenge*, sending a laser signal in the right direction acknowledging.

CS-405 and *Packmule* were twenty light-hours out, hiding in the darkness, talking with their own laser communications rather than radio. Two ugly hunks of rock among all the iceballs and asteroids.

"*Packmule*, this is Phil," his voice came over the line. "Begin your approach now. *CS-405* will take the direct line and be there first. See you on the far side."

Heather turned an expectant eye on Andre.

"It's your mission," he huffed, still unwilling to relax and run with it.

"And you're in command of *Packmule*, Commander," she fired back sweetly.

"Fine," Andre said with just a touch of juvenile whine. "Pilot, execute your jump."

"Executing," Heather laughed. "Remember, this will look good on your resume, one of these days, if you decide you want to command a hospital ship."

"What?" he was shocked.

"Yes," Heather grinned. "Those command centurions are medical personnel with command experience. Like you now."

More grumbling about the unfairness of things. But he didn't have to do or say much at this point. She would plot a course for *Packmule* to escape if something went wrong. She and Veitengruber were likely to be off-ship if that happened, so Andre would be on his own, without a good astrogator.

And he didn't need accuracy. If something went wrong, Andre needed to be gone quickly, so she would throw him as far as the JumpDrives could calculate with any certainty. After that, he could either rendezvous with *CS-405*, or make his own way back to *Lighthouse Station*.

If everything went completely to hell, at least Andre and Bok could make it home.

Hopefully.

"I'm going to go get some coffee," Andre announced with flamboyant sulkiness. "You have the bridge."

Which probably meant that he was going down to the wardroom, where he would get something to eat and remain there for as long as he could get away with, which would be about the time they needed to drop into an orbital slot above *Three*, in such a place that the various gravity wells of all the planets in the neighborhood didn't prevent them from jumping away in a hurry.

And this first jump wouldn't take long. Probably about sixteen minutes, if she read the solar wind and hydrogen density correctly. Piloting inside a system was far slower than deep space, from all the gravity wells you had to maneuver around.

Andre hadn't returned when they dropped into RealSpace, but Heather wasn't surprised or offended. He was a nurse who had been dragooned into doing things far beyond his expertise as a result of possessing a commission. Officer and a Gentleman.

Heather plotted the next jump, smiled, and triggered it as fast as the engines recalibrated.

Bullseye. She smiled at Andre as he wandered back onto the bridge with a mug of coffee and a danish in one hand.

She had intentionally come in a touch high, compared to normal. *Packmule* maneuvered like an iceberg at the best of times, so she wanted the maximum amount of space. It made hiding more difficult, since they had so much less planetary umbra, but that was the cost of doing something this insane.

Anna was supposedly already on the surface, landing at Zone B on Evan's charts. *CS-405* was in an escort position overhead but still below *Packmule*. They would occasionally broach just long enough to listen and peek, to make sure nobody had crashed the party over on *B*.

Heather had both qualified small-craft pilots with her, because of the insertion shuttles, and even then could only really fly two of her three at once. The administrative shuttle on *405* was in the hands of a First-Rate-Spacer busting her ass to get fully certified. The woman almost had enough hours in the trainer and the craft, but she was staying behind.

If something went wrong, *CS-405* was the only one of them with enough shields to escape a hostile warship. Phil risked losing twenty percent of his crew today, down on the surface, so some things were done more carefully than normal.

The rest of them were on their own.

"You have the bridge," Heather announced.

More grumbles.

"And you'll have Dedra, if anything happens," Heather smiled. "I've programmed the big red PANIC button if you need it, along with an estimated course to *Lighthouse Station.*"

"Yes, mother," Andre replied, stumping into the Director's chair and looking for a cupholder.

There wasn't one, but she wasn't going to mention that right now.

Instead, Heather made her way down to the bottom deck, and then forward to the flight bay. Everybody was already suited up for deep space, even though there technically was an atmosphere below them. Nothing they could breathe, and not enough pressure to matter.

She was the last one there, when she emerged in her spacesuit and joined Yamaguchi aboard *Saddlebags.*

"Bridge, this is the flight deck," Veitengruber called over the internal systems. "*Saddlebags* and *Caravan* are ready to launch."

"Clear skies," Andre called back.

Yamaguchi turned to look at her with a question, but Heather just shrugged. No idea what Andre was up to.

Saddlebags was in front, and launched first, a leisurely pass until the other craft joined them, and then a hard, spiraling burn in, centered on the estimated landing zone for *Queen Anne's Revenge.*

Now was when things got sticky.

ZEUS ABOVE (OCTOBER 12, 402)

"Status?" Phil called. He was watching his boards locally, but wanting to hear from Evan and anybody else that needed to have an opinion today.

"Short range laser communications net established and working, sir," Evan said, "We can talk to Andre, both insertion shuttles, and *Queen Anne*. Depending on time and location, they may or may not be able to respond."

"And the ground forces?" Phil continued.

"Confirm three ships on the ground at Zone B," Evan's smile was a little more stern now. "Waiting to hear from them on status."

"Very good," Phil said.

Not much he could do at this point. Except watch and pray. Counting from the moment *Mansi-B* would come above the horizon, they had about a day and a half to work before the two vessels above would have to slide beyond the horizon. The ships and crew on the ground would be exposed, if anyone happened to be looking at this moon with good enough optics to spot three new dots on the ground.

And enough paranoia to be looking.

If that happened, all hell would break loose, and he would probably end up losing twenty percent of his crew in one go. That Court Martial would end his career, regardless of the circumstances.

But if it worked…

"Science Officer, you have Tactical," Phil ordered. "Let's broach and take a look around."

ARCHAEOLOGISTS (OCTOBER 12, 402)

HEATHER LOOKED up at a sky that was the wrong color, and a horizon that was too close. Plus that monster of a planet overhead, a banded marble that dominated the sky like an evil eye.

Three was tidally-locked with its Primary, so the same face was always pointed at the gas giant. That meant that forever, there would be a gigantic moon in the sky, blotting out most of the stars until only a few were visible through the tenuous atmosphere, even as the sun rose and set on a three-day cycle.

She found it easier to keep her head focused on the ground in front of her as she walked, careful not to bounce into the air in the light gravity and go flying away accidentally. Again. Welcome to adventures.

The planet had no magnetic field, so radios were tuned down to the lowest possible broadcast power, in the hopes that nobody would hear them over on the prison world. It was paranoia, but the alternative was worse.

Here, it just meant that anybody inside one of the dead ships was probably out of contact, just because the radios couldn't punch a signal through even that little steel. As a result, she was leading her team over to *Queen Anne's Revenge* on foot, to see what everyone was up to. That team had been on the ground for a day already, and had the ability to drop back down to T-shirts inside the ship.

Sure, the insertion shuttles had airlocks, and heads. And that was about it, unless you wanted to sleep on the hard deck. *Anna* had hammocks that could be slung, and hot showers if you were fast enough. Plus a kitchen.

Heather took a tally of everyone with her. Veitengruber and Yamaguchi, the pilots. Galin and Zubaida as engineers. Vlad and Deni as strong backs. *Anna* had been packed to the gills with folks, so hopefully they had managed to get some work done while they waited for the trucks to arrive. Folks had been working, but she had seen them drifting in this direction as the shuttles came in to land, so this was probably an impromptu afternoon tea, or something.

She went through the airlock with the first group, and found signs on the wall directing her aft and down. With Granville and Ryouichi at her heels, Heather went down to the cargo deck to find helmets arrayed on hooks with names taped on the front. Everyone was still wearing the rest of their space suits, so they expected more work today.

No rest for the wicked.

She joined Siobhan and Kam at the front end of the mob. At least the big repulsor truck was parked outside, so fitting nearly forty people in here was cozy, rather than irritating.

"You last?" Siobhan asked as she got close.

The crowd noise dropped to murmurs.

"One more batch through the airlock and then we're set," Heather said.

Deni led the rest in a few minutes later, and things settled.

"Good news, bad news," Siobhan started off. "None of the ships around here are flight-worthy, right now. Many of them are badly damaged as well, so the amount of effort needed to make them salvageable probably is greater than we want to expend. On the brighter side, all of them were landed, rather than just dumped, so we can get inside them and poke around."

"How about detaching on frames and hauling them off in pieces?" Veitengruber piped up. "The C-type is generally built in three, distinct pieces: bow, body, stern. The insertion shuttles are normally too small to lift something like that, but we're in one-seventh gravity here, so it could be possible."

"Then what?" Kam asked, her engineering sense picking up all sorts of danger signs from the way her nose twitched.

"Then assemble them in orbit," the pilot replied. "At least enough to make it to JumpSpace and go somewhere else where we can fix them."

"Without life support?" Kam asked.

Heather watched the man shrug and remembered he was a pilot, not a line officer. You had to be crazy and semi-suicidal to want to fly snubfighters. That was why she liked the big ships with lots of armor and shielding.

"Life support is contained in the middle section," Granville observed. "Plug engines on the stern and a bridge on the bow, but leave the two ends open to space for now, and a crew could work in both environments for the two weeks it probably takes to sail back to the *Lighthouse*."

Heather nearly laughed out loud when Galin Tuason turned to the pilot with a smile on his face.

"You're nuts, Granvie," he said. "I like you."

The rest of the crew did laugh, so Heather joined in. It was no more insane than any of the other risks they were taking here.

"Heather, since he's yours, I propose leaving you and him here with about half the team," Siobhan continued when the noise had died down. "I'll take *Anna* and the rest to the spot where the D-hulls are marooned, to see if they're in any better shape. Yamaguchi will come with me in *Saddlebags*, and we'll also hope to find any missiles left lying around. Thoughts?"

"We've got about two days until this location is in the shadow, as seen from *Mansi-B*," Heather noted. "Let's spend that time seeing what we can do. After you check the bigger hulls, I need you to touch the third location and see if any of those fighter craft are worth stealing, as well. We've potentially got space to get two or three away, if they can fly, and stuff them aboard both big ships. Better to do it now, since we may not get a second chance at this."

"Right," Siobhan said, pointing at the group in front

of her. "Group flagged as Team-A is with me, so sit tight. Team-B is going with Heather. You've got emergency shelters ready to deploy, and the two shuttles will be on the ground until we load them or get chased off, so it's time for you to suit up and play rock prospectors."

Heather could identify the two groups by the groans and ribbing going back and forth over hot meals and hot showers, something *Anna's* crew would get, while Heather's would be living rough. She made a mental note to ask Granville and Yamaguchi about modifying the third shuttle, the one they flew the least, into something like a recreational vehicle, with showers and a kitchen, for long stakeouts.

Perhaps they should fix one or two containers as troop transports, as well. That might be useful for a hit and fade mission.

"Ladies and gentlemen," Heather said to the group congregating around her. "In case you haven't met him previously, this is Flight Centurion Granville Veitengruber, formerly an Imperial officer, and a *Holding* Slave. He'll be calling the shots as we go look into stealing a warship for Phil."

PROSPECTOR (OCTOBER 12, 402)

GRANVILLE COULDN'T HELP the blush. He had not been expecting Captain Lau to introduce him to the group that way. Nor to hold him up as the decision-maker about their collective future, stealing back Imperial warships so they could return them to duty.

But Deni smiled at him from one side of the group, and that was what he needed. Another outsider being welcomed here.

Chief Engineer Rushforth was joining this team. His team. She was a Senior Centurion, the same as Captain Lau, but both were deferring to his experience and authority, whatever of it there actually was left, after seven years on a prison farm.

"What do we know?" he asked Rushforth as an opener.

She had been on the ground for a day already, so she had to have crawled through all of them, looking at damage and assessing reparability.

"There are four here in reasonable shape," she said. "Plus two others that had suffered significant damage, but one of those appeared to be an engine detonation that took out the rear of the ship, and the other appeared to have taken a direct hit forward, possibly losing everything to that first major frame, if they are truly built in thirds."

"I have been studying *Aquitaine* ships," he said with a grin. "At least as much as my current security clearance allows. Your ships, pardon, *our* ships are built with more frames, and less standardization. *Fribourg* vessels tend to be cookie-cutter designs. In the case of the cutters, rather than building a new ship, it would be possible to remove and salvage any lost third, and replace it with newer equipment. Not necessarily cheaper, in the long run, but much faster to build and repair, and it allows the entire fleet to be slowly upgraded in place, rather than build new hulls and retire perfectly serviceable old ones."

"That would explain something Phil suggested about *Buran*, but wasn't the case on the ground," Heather said. "He said he was expecting two of any design captured, to make sure that one wasn't a one-off design, if you needed to go back and inspect them later."

Granville watched the nods. It made perfect sense. For cruisers, that was exactly what would happen. Frigates, to a lesser extent, but the E-hulls would also tend to be standardized on a single design and then dozens or hundreds of them decanted.

D-type hulls and below tended to be a much more random selection of things. Hopefully, that would work to his advantage.

"If so, then that explains keeping six," Granville

grinned. "And Captain Skokomish will encounter something similar when she goes to look at the site with the D-type hulls, although those tend to be done in quarters, rather than thirds."

"Is that why they're a third bigger?" Yeoman Tuason asked, a little metaphorical light bulb coming on over his head. "You build them all in the same yard and just assemble different pieces as you go?"

"Indeed," Granville acknowledged with a fierce grin. "It allows shipyards to standardize as well, so C- and D-hulls can be put out from the same line, as needed."

"And you think we can pull them apart on the ground?" Kam asked, somewhat incredulous.

"As I said earlier," he replied mildly. "The gravity here is one-seventh. But the insertion shuttle and the transport truck both have winch capabilities, so I believe we might be able to dismantle sections, and then lift them, or possibly reassemble them on the ground."

The Chief Engineer fixed him with a hard stare for several seconds before she finally spoke.

"Galin's correct, Veitengruber," she said. "You are nuts. But it might work, and we can always bring in *Anna* and the other shuttle if we need extra lifting capacity."

"Very good, sir," he said, "Then we need to go look at the relics and see if we can commit mayhem."

Somehow, he ended up in the first group to exit the airlock, down the external stairs, and across the dusty ground. There was enough atmosphere to have wind, mostly driven by convection from the star, and a little off of the gas giant. Reports from Centurion Brinich had suggested some additional level of volcanic activity, location currently unknown, but likely to be discovered, if *CS-405* spent several days in low orbit, hiding in the planetary umbra and scanning the ground for more prospecting sites.

Granville Veitengruber had always sneered down his nose at the crews of the police cutters. As a young, mouthy, hotshot fighter pilot, he had frequently had more offensive capacity in his *A-6j* fighter than one of these C-type hulls. And a higher spot in the social pecking order.

Seven years as a slave had knocked most of those edges off his soul. These ships had not gone to *Samara* with a fleet to beat back the invaders. Fleet took nothing smaller than D-class hulls, and those only as escorts for carriers, which told him that these ships had been captured somewhere else.

Most likely from *Buran* raids? Captain Lau hadn't mentioned any, except to suggest that perhaps *Fribourg* had not been particularly forthcoming with certain embarrassing information.

He could see that. Who wanted to admit that they could not defend their own worlds? And yet, wasn't that exactly what Admiral Kosnett was attempting to do? *Holding* warships could not be captured, with the notable exception of what Admiral Keller had apparently managed with surprise and something called a Heavy Dreadnaught.

Granville followed the Chief Engineer as she stalked her prey. The dust here was almost orange, a mix of iron, carbon, and silicates that looked like an ugly, endless beach under an eternally-sunsetting sky with a dread-bringing cat's-eye in the sky overhead.

Heather Lau walked with the Chief Engineer, and

Deni strode at his side. It made a nicely balanced picture. Two fierce naval officers. Two ex-slaves still trying to figure out what freedom might taste like.

Rushforth's first target was the one that had gotten its nose punched in by something bigger, meaner, and angrier. Not that hard, in a C-type cutter, when almost anything else in space qualified.

The ship was flat on its belly in the sand, rather than resting on landing skids, like the four others in better shape. Someone, presumably one of Rushforth's engineers, had forced an airlock aft, but Granville steered the group forward, counting steps against his memory of naval college midshipman cruises, over a decade ago.

He found the spot that marked the first major frame. It was obvious to the naked eye when he got there, where scouring winds had stripped off the electroplating that protected the ship against solar wind. Two rings, each about a meter thick, pressed up against each other and running a complete circumference around the ship.

Yes, the join spot.

Yeoman Tuason was close by, so Granville grabbed the man and touched face plates with him briefly.

"Find me an airlock forward of this spot," he ordered the young man, pointing at the frame line in the hull.

Tuason nodded and approached the hull, while Granville stepped back to try to envision the whole of the ship. Four decks in total, with the top and bottom pinching in on the sides and a central hallway, and the two decks in the middle having two corridors running fore to aft.

Daylight caught his eye and Granville stepped a little

to his right. The damage in the hull made sense now. Something had hit the hull hard enough to punch a hole cleanly through. Given the shape of the external hull plates visible, the shot had been coming at him from port, and exited through the starboard side, right where he was looking.

And if he had counted his steps correctly, it had passed almost exactly through the tiny ship's bridge. Larger ships might survive and continue fighting, but C-type hulls only had one control space. Lose that, and you lost the ability to see, fly, or fight.

Battle over, and quickly. Ship captured and carried off to examine it to see if it had any military secrets worth noting. And given the damage, the forward turret was possibly too badly damaged to even consider, but he would have one of the engineers look at it anyway. This piece would be lighter to haul to space, with a core punched out of it like a giant apple. Easier to access the weapon space, perhaps.

Tuason found a spot and cranked the forward airlock open by hand. It was normally at the bottom of the door, but that presumed the ship was landed normally, instead of being dumped. Here, it was about at his shoulder level, which would make climbing in interesting, since everybody would misjudge the jump in low gravity.

But the man got it open quickly enough. Rushforth and Lau let him lead at this point, with Tuason, *Galin*, staying close by.

Granville really was in charge. At least as much as he wanted to be.

The ship was dark, but their suits had lights. Dust had

blown into these hallways over time, which told him that the kill had been fast and efficient, and nothing forward of this frame had probably survived.

He found himself on a sunlit bridge, cursing the bastards that had ambushed a helpless police cutter and killed it. Probably a Mako chomping down on a helpless guppy.

But he was correct about the forward turret. It might be more easily salvageable, depending on the other ships. That would give them an extra gun they could consider mounting on *CS-405* to replace one of the defense turrets, if Admiral Kosnett chose that path.

Aft, the tale was different. The first frame had held, from the looks of things. Again, that made sense if a shark suddenly dropped out of jump on top of you and fired a bullet through your ship's brain. The rest of the corpse might still be pretty.

"Thoughts?" Captain Lau asked over the radio after he had spent several minutes tinkering around and looking over Galin's shoulder.

"The bow is a loss," Granville replied. "Stern two-thirds appear to be in reasonable shape. I want to consider separating the bow and taking it, anyway, though. The weapon might be repairable, and taking a bow third missing so much mass would make it easier to lift."

"Noted," she said, neither agreeing nor disagreeing with his assessment.

There were still five more corpses to look at.

CORONER (OCTOBER 13, 402)

GRANVILLE SAT on a handy landing skid and let the ship take his weight. Even in one-seventh gravity, he had done more work today than he could remember, at least since calving last spring.

If time was no pressure, there were probably three ships that could be assembled from mismatched parts. All that required was turning the surface of this moon into a petite dry-dock and bringing in a few overhead cranes that could move this sort of mass.

He watched a light appear on the too-near horizon and approach, resolving itself into *Queen Anne's Revenge* and landing on the far side of his insertion shuttle, *Saddlebags* in her wake.

Over the last nine hours, he had walked, climbed, squatted, and cursed the other five derelicts, touching each section in turn and consulting with Galin, Heather, and Kam about the relative merits of each.

Number one was still his favorite, even laying in the

sand rather than resting on skids like the rest. Three and four had fought back before being taken. They had suffered damage across much of their hulls, and probably had internal systems that would require too much love and time to fix. Number two had indeed suffered some manner of engine failure, catastrophically and in sequence. The outer hull had peeled back from the aft forward, as though the explosion had been contained by the hull and the frame, with everything in the middle melted and shredded.

At the same time, the bow of the second ship looked almost pristine. Granville would have guessed that the last section was the oldest, and should have been replaced when the bow was, then not too long after that trouble had come for them and they had been destroyed at the moment they brought everything on line.

Five and six had nothing particularly interesting or flawed about them. But they were the oldest ones here. As with two and three, damage was spread across all sections, but not so bad that it couldn't be repaired.

Given time.

Granville looked up in surprise when a hand landed on his shoulder. Deni smiled down at him.

Heather had knelt in front of him when he wasn't looking, putting their eyes about on a plane.

"As your commanding officer, I have one thing to say," she muttered. "How the hell are you still able to keep going, after all that?"

A hand gestured at the half-dozen corpses lined up for the coroner to inspect. Granville realized that time on a cattle ranch had given him and Deni far deeper reserves of endurance than a naval officer on active duty might have. He considered that the marines under Trinidad Mildon might be the only other crew members that could have easily kept up today.

He grinned at her.

"Calves don't care how many hours you've been awake, Commander," he replied. "They're coming, and coming now, and you better be there to help."

"Ugh," she groaned, rising slowly to her feet. "I intend to claim seniority and take the first shower after the briefing. Shall we?"

Granville rose as well.

"Break time," he called over the team channel.

Everyone was in sight at this point, many of them collapsed against hulls and skids from the effort of the last day. Granville still had more pep, so he ended up in the first batch of crew through the airlock, simply because his feet weren't dragging. Deni and Heather joined him, along with Galin and one of the crew he didn't immediately know on sight yet.

Up, through, aft, down. This ship wasn't designed with an airlock on the cargo deck. Instead, the assumption was that it would dock against a station, establish a seal against the hull, and lower the front hatch as a ramp.

Crew inside were already in hammocks slung around the outer walls when he got there. He found Captain Skokomish and several of her crew seated on handy boxes and jumpseats, but Markus Dunklin was the man he really wanted to talk to.

"Four hulls?" Granville asked as he got close. "How were they?"

Markus looked up with bloodshot eyes. The man might have been awake for two days, with only catnaps. That was okay. Everybody would sleep for a while now, as the leaders figured out their next course of action.

"One of them is probably only worth melting down for metals," Dunklin said. "Two got scragged pretty good in battle, but look like they could still fly. One of them looks almost cherry."

It took Granville a moment to place the euphemism. From the Mongolian everyone was speaking, it translated into English as something rather rude. But he got the gist of it.

"Fuel on the last one?" he asked.

"Drained, but it looked like the ship was powered down cleanly and winterized, for lack of a better term. Didn't bring it live, but we could have, tapping the tanks on *Saddlebags*. Didn't feel right, if that makes any sense?"

Granville smiled. Markus and Galin were what Heather and the commanders called rednecks. Both would have settled right in on that ranch without much fuss. You had to make do with what you had, rather than cursing what you didn't. And adapt things to do tasks they were never intended for, when that was all you had.

"I suspect it was a trap," Granville said. "A honey pot."

Even tired, Dunklin's eyes lit up with savage anger.

"Yes," he said. "Too perfect. That's why it felt wrong."

"Explanation, in small words, please?" Heather asked.

She, Siobhan, and Kam had perked up, arrayed to one side while Granville and Galin talked to Markus.

"Let's envision some sort of escape from the prison world," Granville said, pitching his voice loud enough that some of the others around the room could hear. "A stealthy rocket or something without JumpDrives, but capable of getting you to space. A few men, rather than a bunch."

"Sure," Heather nodded, unsure where he was going.

"There are captured warships in the LaGrange orbits of *Mansi-B*, but those are large vessels, requiring crews of scores or perhaps hundreds to operate," Granville continued. "But you know that there smaller ships parked over here, so you race over and look for something that can escape. Most people would be crew off of bigger vessels, so they would gravitate towards the D-type hulls. Police cutters are frequently the lowest rung on the social ladder in *Fribourg*'s Fleet, as I can attest."

He paused to examine his audience. Most of the folks awake were listening. Probably the ones asleep as well, since that was a skill every sailor learned early.

"So you land, and find a D-type hull in miraculously-perfect shape, requiring only fuel and you can escape forever, bringing down the terrible angels of vengeance on this planet," he said, letting his voice range out of simple explanation and take on some storytelling elements. "You fuel it from your first ship, power everything on, and take off."

"And the damned thing explodes on you as soon as you light the engines, doesn't it?" Dunklin asked.

"I would not put it past them," Granville said. "Especially since all the other ships we have found have been in such poor shape. A Trojan Horse, in reverse, if you will. What were the missile magazines like?"

"Full," Dunklin hissed. "Fourteen birds that looked like they were in good shape."

"All the better," Granville growled. "Wouldn't you want such a grand ship to help you get home?"

"Where's the bomb?" Markus growled back.

"It could be anywhere," Granville admitted. "Maybe an engine overload. Maybe a generator with a failsafe disabled. Possibly the missiles in the tubes will detonate in place, setting off a chain reaction. If we had forever, we could take the ship apart and find it. When we come back, we will. But it's not worth looking today."

"What are your suggestions, Centurion?" Heather asked in an interested voice.

Technically, it was her mission. Her job. Her command. But she was, as the saying went, willing to sell him as much rope as he wanted to buy.

And Granville was feeling awfully greedy today.

"Fourteen missiles in the racks?" he asked.

"Plus five more in the other hulls," Markus replied, tiredness suddenly wiped clean. His eyes even looked brighter. "Like those bastards emptied as many as they needed, in order to reload the trap for us."

Granville turned to Heather, Siobhan, and Kam, the engineers suddenly witnesses, but not central agents.

"Remove all the missiles and get them into the containers on *Saddlebags*," he said. "Yamaguchi swaps for *Highway* and flies it down for the second run. We try to strip as much gear as we can from the carcasses, while the other team puts together a C-type hull from parts to give us a second warship. We don't get greedy at that point, instead sailing off to *Lighthouse Station* and caching as much as we can there. At some point, we either attempt a prison break, or run for Imperial Space and get help."

"Then why the missiles?" Heather asked.

"They're just as useful blowing up a station somewhere else," Granville said, his voice rising. "Same Trojan Horse gambit with an insertion shuttle. Maybe we go find a luxury liner or an empty troop transport and bring it back here."

"Are you too angry or tired to make rational decisions, Centurion?" she fired back. It was like cold water on his neck.

"No," he said after a moment of consideration. "Those men have been sentenced to death under an alien sun, Commander. Slow death, perhaps, but they are never going home, unless we build a yellow-brick-road for them. How many thousands of men do you suppose have disappeared from Imperial space over the last two generations?"

"Too many," she agreed. "But I want you calm, rational, and deadly. Having a second warship means that Phil can extend his campaign across a wider front. Or it means that we can run for home and get help. But he'll make that decision."

She turned to include more of the group. Everyone was indoors now, helmets off and listening.

"Everyone eats now, and then racks for eight hours," she ordered the room. "Tomorrow, Siobhan, Kam, Granville, and I are going to work you like dogs."

Granville nodded at the general groans from the room.

Tomorrow, was going to be a significant step forward.

He had seven years of misery that he owed someone.

INTRUDER (OCTOBER 14, 402)

"All hands to battle stations," the voice came through the speaker by the hatch, boosting Phil up out of his sleep cycle and towards the hatch before he was even fully awake. He grabbed his tunic from the chair at the foot of the bed and slid his feet into shoes, and then exited his cabin at nearly a dead run.

It wasn't far to the bridge from the Command Centurion's cabin, by design, but he didn't want to stop even long enough to put on his tunic. He could do that when he was on station.

Yeoman Lovisone had the watch right now. Good pilot, damned fine sailor. Not ready to engage in a war without some serious backup.

"West, what's the situation?" Phil called to the man as he entered the bridge.

He threw himself into his station and powered all the boards live. Sensors had been left in passive mode for days, drinking from the river of data without adding any ripples to the water. All four gun crews showed green, as much good as that would do. If someone was coming, *405* would probably have to run, rather than fight. Still, the crew was tight, even as short-handed as they were running right now.

"Signal from the top edge of the system, sir," West called. "New vessel just jumped into a spot directly above *Mansi-B* from somewhere. Signal's several hours old at this point, so hopefully he dropped down into *B*'s orbit and we just haven't seen him yet."

Phil considered the scenario. It sounded reasonable, except that this was a prison planet, and a secret one. He suspected that the newcomer was parked out there waiting permission to close, instead of just appearing on the horizon.

Still, the boards showed it, sitting about five light-hours out, exactly north from *Mansi-B*, so they knew where they were going. Hopefully, he was just a small asteroid in *Mansi-D*'s vicinity from where the intruder was.

That was the problem with JumpSpace. You could move around faster than signals intelligence could keep up, Noise you emitted rippled outward at light speed, ghosts appearing and disappearing on scanners. *CS-405* might not know they'd been spotted until someone emerged on top of them and opened fire.

Phil double-checked, but West hadn't raised shields. Those were the standing orders that only he or Evan could override, but sometimes your training took over and automatic actions happened.

Here, that would get them seen. And then things would get bad.

Worse, he wasn't over the landing site right now. *405* and *Packmule* were below the horizon from Heather and Siobhan for another seven hours.

He opened a line to the other ship as he pulled his tunic on and sealed it.

"*Packmule*, this is Kosnett," he said, his voice a little quieter than normal, even though they were speaking on a direct laser that should be impossible to detect. "What is your status?"

"Hands poised over the magic button," Andre Gave replied immediately. "Awaiting orders."

"Stay quiet for now," Phil said. "If anything jumps over here, run as soon as you detect their emergence. In a pinch, Siobhan can fly the ground crew out, and Heather can navigate the big beast back down for a second run if we get one."

"Affirmative, Phil," Andre said. "Heather left me a plot that gets me back to Bok, in case the worst happens."

"Roger that," Phil said. "Stand by."

He cut the line and watched his boards as the data got processed. Evan came through the hatch at a dead run, sliding into his station and punching buttons rapidly, speeding up information flow.

According to the data they had, a Hammerhead had just come out of jump. Well, five hours ago. Their next jump should put them close in to *Mansi-B*, if *405* and *Packmule* went undetected. With all externals turned off, they should be invisible to anybody not pinging this immediate vicinity hard.

There, *Buran* had something of an edge. A Hammerhead was an escort vessel, about the size of the old destroyer *Sofia* he had served on, fresh out of school. Half again bigger than *CS-405*, and several times more heavily-armed, but the ships also had some scouting capabilities.

Buran used Hammerheads as jacks of all trades: escorts, scouts, patrol. Hopefully, the Director over there wasn't paranoid enough to look at the junkyard before sailing to his destination.

"Evan, West, on emergence of any vessel, bring shields to full power immediately," Phil ordered. "Gun crews, as soon as you have a target, open fire with everything you've got."

As pitifully small as that might be. Still, they might get lucky. And luck counted for more than skill in almost any game, war included.

Green lights.

Phil settled in to wait. There wasn't anything he could do at this point, except hope he got lucky.

EFFICIENCY.

Phil had to give them that. The intruder had sat patiently out there. Five hours had passed since he had appeared on sensors. Long enough for a message from *Mansi-B* to get back out to him. He then appeared just outside the gravity well edge of *Mansi-B*, just about where an *Aquitaine* squadron would have.

Phil suspected the Director of the Hammerhead was

following orders, and had dropped exactly into the center of a killing zone. That's where all *his* guns would have optimized, if he was in command over there.

CS-405 was slightly broached, just peeking out from the bottom of *Three*. That sort of piloting worked to their advantage, too. *Buran* tended to fly above solar systems and enter them from the north, whereas *Aquitaine* flew in direct lines as much as possible.

Jessica Keller had taught the squadron to stay south as much as possible, and that tended to hide them better.

It had apparently worked here.

As Phil watched, the Hammerhead intruder slowly made its way in towards the closest station and docked.

Evan had tentatively marked that one as belonging to the commander of the system, based on the amount of signals traffic emanating from it, compared to the other seven.

It would be Phil's target, if they ever launched a surprise attack.

"*Packmule*, this is *405*," Phil said, opening a line.

It had to suck over there, with only two crew on the vessel right now and having to do everything, while still staying ready to run at the first sign of trouble.

"Janowski," the engineer replied. "Andre's taking a nap. Should I wake him?"

"Negative, Dedra," Phil said. "Intruder has docked with the station, so you can relax some. Unless they crash jump from the dock itself, we'll have a few minutes warning between the time we see them undock and the time they could get to a normal jump location. Next time, remind me to send a couple of spare folks over so you can keep better sleep schedules."

"That would be nice, boss," Dedra replied.

Nobody had considered that with only two people on the ship, they would end up on twelve and twelve schedules at a minimum, cut even shorter when something went wrong.

Like now.

Two hours until he had a direct line to the ground and could feed them an update. At least nobody down there was going to move, without a notice from him. Hopefully, he didn't have to overfly them at high speed, warning them of an intruder at the same time that he was leading the hounds right over their location.

MECHANIC (OCTOBER 14, 402)

THE JOY of impact wrenches and prybars, as Granville surveyed the scene from the cockpit of *Caravan*. Galin and Markus had gone at the wreck of number one with a vengeance, once he showed them how to identify the panels covering the twenty-centimeter bolts holding the two frames together.

Kam and a handful of others had used a stack of stolen bar and beam stock to build a crane-like attachment on the middle section. It wouldn't allow them to lift the ship, but it would let them control things.

Heather turned and faced him across the vast yard, both hands up, just in case he wasn't paying attention to the woman.

"*Caravan*, stand by," she said over the short range radio.

Heavy cables had been strung under the front section of the derelict and laced together like a net, passing through rings welded on first thing this morning.

"All set," Granville replied, confirming that nothing had moved off center on any gauge in the last thirty seconds.

"*Caravan*, begin your lift," Heather continued. "Bear your nose on me and then prepare to walk forward."

Here was the time when an insertion shuttle showed its value over anything short of a tugboat. Pure maneuverability. Granville eased the controller up a hair at a time, bringing the ship up onto its toes, and then lifting clear of the ground.

Up a meter. Two. Five and hold.

He set the autopilot to maintain this distance from the ground and slowly rotated himself counterclockwise until Heather was in line with where guns could parallax, if he had any.

Her hands began to move, a complex signaling language he had taught her, based on what he had learned from his old flight crews, and from a bunch of Mongolian cowboys needing to herd restive cattle.

He approached her at a slow walk. There was no breeze today, so it was easier than normal. Almost like docking in orbit, where the only thing you had to address was relative closure rates.

Her hands crossed overhead, and Granville eased into a clean hover. The repulsors kicked up a little dust, but not much, as they had selected a rocky flat to try this from first.

"Cable crew, begin your approach," Heather called over the radio.

Granville cycled one of his screens to show the underside of the shuttle. Three engineers dragged hooked cables under the ship and attached them to a ring specifically engineered to be the lowest center of gravity, so that an insertion shuttle could lift a massive weight without tilting.

He would have never dared a stunt like this in an administrative shuttle.

One, two, three hooks attached and locked, and the crew backed away quickly.

"*Caravan*, this is your Ground Controller," Heather continued in a heavy, serious voice. "Prepare to maneuver."

"Acknowledged, *Ground Control*," Granville said.

Now, things got tricky.

Markus's truck was parked in a line with the bow of the derelict, several cables attached to the front winch. Markus would do the pulling, but Granville had to lift the entire weight of the front end and hold everything steady while the redneck worked.

"Forward ten, up twenty, *Caravan*," Heather ordered.

"Forward ten, up twenty," Granville acknowledged.

Forward slowly, lifting to a programmed height of twenty-five meters. He could trust the shuttle's computer to handle that part. What came after required human intervention. It would all be touch.

"Hold there, *Caravan*," Heather said.

Granville looked at the image from below. Three cables as thick as his thigh bones hung down, but remained loose yet. One on each side of the target, just forward from the frame lines. The last one hooked to where a bowsprit would have been, had this been a maritime ship.

"*Caravan*, forward two, and adjust for a five kph drift from starboard," Heather ordered.

Not much breeze, but enough to push him sideways, ever so slightly.

"*Caravan*, you appear to be centered," Heather said. "Confirm."

Down view looked good. All cables appeared to have the same amount of slack. Autopilot was holding him as close to mathematical center as they had been able to identify.

"Ground Control, this is *Caravan*," Granville said. "Confirm centering."

"Begin your lift, *Caravan*," she ordered. "Slow and steady."

Back on the controller using the buttons on the screen, rather than the stick itself. One tap at a time, measured in decimeters of altitude.

The ship groaned a little as the cables came taut. He added one last tap and held it there. The front of the ship would probably shift a little, if they held this for an hour, but for now, the weight would be mostly off of the bolts.

"Ground Control, I have positive hold," Granville said.

"Stand by, *Caravan*," she answered. "Towtruck, begin to take in your slack."

Granville watched the winch on Markus's truck turn very slowly, pulling those cables in and winding them.

Contact.

Two musical instruments in the afternoon sun, one horizontal, one vertical.

"Ground Control, all slack taken in," Markus called in a heavy voice.

"*Caravan*, take me up one-tenth and hold," Heather ordered carefully.

Granville eased the autopilot up another notch. He couldn't see a difference below, but the engines beneath him revved at a higher pitch with the extra effort.

"Hold there, *Caravan*," she called. "Towtruck, apply positive pressure now."

"Initiating," Markus answered.

They had anchored the truck to the ground with spikes driven more than a meter into the rock, but Granville still watched those cables come tight as the winch pulled.

"Spotters, give me an update," Heather called.

"One, negative," Galin answered.

"Two, negative," Zubaida chimed in a moment later.

No movement from the ship. That was always the risk with something like this. The ship might have flash-welded at the seam when it was hit. Or somehow rusted internally.

They just might not be able to break it loose.

"Ground Control, this is *Caravan*," Granville said as he looked at the situation. "Stand by. I want to try something."

"What's coming, *Caravan*?"

"I will try to rock it loose vertically, Ground Control," he said.

"Be careful," Heather ordered.

"Will do."

Granville eased the autopilot up another notch. Nothing moved, but the lifters changed pitch.

Down two blips.

Up two blips.

The machine had a lag built in. It had just started to ease off when the second command hit and the engines surged. The symphony around him wasn't an opera, but it wasn't experimental jazz, either.

"Two, I have movement," Zubaida called suddenly.

"Negative on one, still," Galin answered.

"Everybody on your toes," Granville ordered. "I'm going to rock it sideways a little."

"Don't shear any bolts, *Caravan*," Heather said.

He grinned. The only bolts he was likely to shear were on his shuttle, not the cutter below him.

Okay, now it got interesting. Small crosswind. Cables as tight as a violin.

Granville took both sticks in hand. He would have to do this by touch. The computer wasn't fast enough for his needs.

Deep breath. Settle everything into the earth and become the shuttle you are flying.

He cut the autopilot and held the ship perfectly still, except for the heartbeat echoing through his fingertips on the control sticks. It was only a little crazy right now.

More to come.

Granville slid left and down. This was the human element. An autopilot computer didn't have the subtlety to cut a clean chord of arc. Rather, it would stair-step down and over.

That would shear off something. Probably a cable

holding him, in which case he might turn turtle before he could react.

Now, subtle. Soft. Easy.

Drift until the system fights you and back off.

Up and over and down the other side of the hill.

Ignore your racing heartbeat. You are an Imperial pilot, serving your Emperor to the best of your ability. You are an Officer and a Gentleman.

Touch and tug.

Reverse. Up and over. Down and out.

Tap like cutting a diamond.

"One, I have movement," Galin yelled.

"Two, confirm movement," Zubaida answered.

"*Caravan*, stabilize now," Heather ordered.

"Roger that, Ground Control," he breathed, letting the adrenaline flow out with his breath, since he couldn't let go to do it with his hands.

Granville centered again, felt the three cables come into harmony in a way they hadn't before. A violin, perfectly tuned.

"Towtruck, you are go," Heather called.

The cables pulled a little and then Granville felt the entire edifice shift in his fingertips. He was a balloon now, in a child's hands at the park, as Markus slowly pulled the massive bow towards the truck.

"One, I have daylight," Galin called.

"Two, confirm daylight," Zubaida replied.

"Towtruck, pulling them clear," Markus answered.

Granville thought he could feel Markus's heartbeat through the cables as the truck began to tug, like pulling taffy before it cooled.

Big silver balloon in the park.

Something snapped loose as the front section cleared the bolts holding it. Granville felt the wind take hold of the bow section and begin to push it sideways, like a kitten rubbing at his ankles.

"We're clear," Heather yelled to everyone. "Towtruck, pull him another five meters and then stop."

"Five and hold," Markus replied. "We're there and holding."

"*Caravan*, begin your drift," Heather orchestrated. "Lean to starboard and drift around the chord until I hold you."

Granville adjusted the controls, moving like mud sliding across the field. He could feel where the truck was anchoring him, a human with a small terrier straining on his leash in the park.

"*Caravan*, stand by," Heather came over the line. "Towtruck, begin slacking your line now."

Granville felt the leash loosen, letting him rush over to sniff the new plant and see who had come by in the last few days. The harmonics below him shifted as the line loosened and he drifted some more.

"Towtruck, hold there," Heather called.

Suddenly, the leash was taught again, keeping him just short of a kibble that had fallen on the carpet where he couldn't quite reach it.

"*Caravan*, you are clear to set your weight down," Heather continued. "Everyone is clear."

Granville let the stick slide forward just a little, moving like a feather to the ground. The harmony changed as the lines slacked.

"*Caravan*, lower one and hold there," Heather ordered.

Granville brought the shuttle down a little more and engaged the autopilot, letting the computer hold them for now. The stress in his shoulders finally released as he let the tension bleed out.

"*Caravan*, I need you to come back ten and down ten," Heather ordered.

"Back ten and down ten," Granville replied, touching the buttons and letting the ship drift back into the new spot.

"*Caravan*, back eight more and then drop to five meters elevation."

Fingertips moved automatically as the ship relaxed almost as much as Granville did.

There was a long pause as he hovered in place.

"Okay, *Caravan*," Heather called. "Down three and hold there for ground crew."

It was like they had done this every day of their lives, as he brought the ship down and the stevedores slid underneath him to detach the three hooks and their cables from his belly button.

Granville watched them on the screen like the vessel was an extension of his being. Suddenly, he was back in his fighter craft in the old days, back to the magic he could pull in the days before *Samara* changed everything.

"*Caravan*, you are flying free," Heather said. "Good job and return to your landing zone."

He felt like a dragonfly, moving in three dimensions automatically and landing on his skids with a feather touch.

Granville powered things down as fast as he could and

moved out the side hatch. He wanted to see it with his eyes, rather than the cameras. Something just felt different that way.

He locked through and stepped into the early morning sun of *Three*.

The target ship was a third shorter now, missing the bow on a clean cylinder. And he hadn't had to overheat anything getting the bow section clear, so they ought to be able to rig a proper net and lift it to orbit, where Kam's crew could get in and take out the Type-3 beam that would make the whole extra effort worthwhile.

"Damned nice flying, Granvie," Heather said as he emerged to find her close by. "Add that to the resume, if a naval career turns out to be something you don't want to pursue. Anybody that flies a crane like that will never lack for work."

"Thank you, Commander," Granville replied, blushing inside his helmet.

Deni was there as well, silent, but his smile meant everything in the world.

Markus and Galin were standing in the spot where the bow had been removed, so Granville moved over to see what they saw.

A big hole in the sand. But one filled with promise. If everything went well, they could just lift another bow section off and settle it into place here, letting the ground hold it in place while they lined up the bolts.

Trying this on any of the ships on skids would have required that they build up a cradle for it, and hope it held up, or lower the damned thing to the ground like they had here.

Galin gave him a big thumbs up as they finished a visual inspection of the bolts sticking out. None visually cracked or bent under the stress, so they could move forward.

Kam walked over and touched helmet face plates with him. She didn't say anything, just smiled, so it was more of a friendly thing, like athletes patting each other on the bottom.

Granville felt an enormous energy in his stomach that he couldn't name, but it was powerful and warm.

"You want the bow off two or six?" Kam finally asked, this time over the radio. "Those are the best, and I can't see any major difference between the two."

He finally had a name for that feeling. It had been absent for so long, that he had forgotten what it was.

Granville Veitengruber *belonged*. He was home.

"How hard would it be to drag the bow across the sand, rather than lowering it into place?" he asked.

She turned and looked at the situation. Markus and Galin had heard the question, so they joined in.

By the second sentence, Granville had gotten completely lost, as the conversation delved into obscure and arcane vocabulary absolutely over his head. He turned to Heather and Siobhan, but they both shrugged silently.

Experts doing their thing.

After a few minutes, the threesome achieved some consensus, at least according to their body language. At least he thought so.

"Bow two," Kam announced. "We'll do the same thing that we did here and slide it close. Then we'll flip everything around and pull it down."

"Why not put some pulleys on the middle section and then drag it into contact without moving the truck?" Granville asked. "I can hold the hover reasonably well if I don't have to do more than keep it light while dragging across the ground."

From the way Galin smiled and preened, he had asked the same question, and possibly been overruled. But Kam and Siobhan and Heather had put him in charge.

Maybe he was pulling rank? Was that allowed, for an ex-Imperial, ex-slave, junior officer?

"We could," Kam allowed. "You'll be doing that for maybe an hour, depending, rather than five minutes. Can you?"

"The autopilot was doing most of the work, Chief," he said. "I only had to step in when we needed to rock it clear. Nothing more when we go for the next section."

"All right," Kam nodded. "Everybody take a break and get some food in you. Then a quick nap and some caffeine and we'll start the next stage."

"Ground team, this is *CS-405*," a voice suddenly overrode everything. "Burst message transmitted. Analyze and respond."

And then nothing.

Burst message meant a text file had been transmitted, along with a lot of pictures, but that they needed to make it quick, so the line could close without giving the ship away in orbit.

Heather and Siobhan shared a glance as Granville watched, and then took off across the field at a dead run for *Queen Anne's Revenge*. Kam and Markus were a step behind them, but Galin had stayed with Granville, next to the derelict.

The engineer looked over expectantly.

"They'll handle it, Galin," Granville said. "Let's figure out what we need to do to get that other bow over here before we run out of time."

Galin nodded and began to trot over to the second ship. Granville followed close behind. Admiral Kosnett wouldn't have sent something like that unless there were problems in orbit.

In that case, *Packmule* would vanish immediately, and their only hope of escaping would be aboard *Queen Anne's Revenge*.

Unless they had their own warship ready to come out fighting.

HEATHER WAS in the left hand seat, across from Siobhan. Kam was in the hatchway with Markus. Outside, the rest of the crew was still at work with whatever they had been doing earlier. If time was up, they would abandon everything in a moment, but until then, they all had work that needed doing.

The screen lit up with an orbital plot animation, with Phil's voice as a narrator.

"At present, a Hammerhead had entered the system and docked with the primary station orbiting *Mansi-B*," Phil intoned seriously. "We do not believe that they have spotted us at present, or they would have already come to investigate. All of this occurred while you were in the period of radio silence three hours ago. Right now, *CS-405* and *Packmule* are maintaining their vigilance, as we do not know if this is a normal pattern for a sector patrol ship, a special message being delivered relating to increased piracy, or perhaps a prisoner being transported. Given the circumstances, you are ordered to do two things. I appreciate that they are absolutely contrary, and I'm smiling as you roll your eyes at me when I tell you to deal with it anyway."

Phil paused there. Heather assumed Evan's maniacal giggling had been edited out of the audio track.

Probably.

"Standing order number one: You are to prepare for emergency lift-off on two-minutes notice. I appreciate that you will have to consolidate your efforts to one site, since only *Anna* will be able to get you to safety if a problem does arise. Standing order number two: You are not to lift from the surface without an emergency until *CS-405* has given you an all-clear notice, from either myself or Evan. If they don't see us, you'll have that much longer to complete whichever task you deem to be most important. If you complete your first task, you can move on to subsequent jobs, as long as you remain in compliance with order number one. I won't ask if there are any questions, because we will be maintaining radio silence forward. You may record a burst response and send to orbit in an hour when we will maneuver to be directly overhead. Please keep the profanities professional and to as much of a minimum as you can. Phil Kosnett, commanding."

"I got a few profanities for you, Phil," Heather muttered under her breath.

Siobhan snorted and killed the line.

"Maybe we should moon the camera in unison and send it up to him?" Kam asked.

"There's always that," Heather laughed. "Siobhan, I'll

let you call Yamaguchi and get them headed over here as quickly as we can. I'll go brief the rest."

"Should we pull one of the containers with missiles aboard Markus's truck and stash it in the cargo hold?" Siobhan asked. "Just in case we have to abandon the two insertion shuttles on the ground."

"Yes, do that," Heather ordered, adjusting all her tactical planning now that all her other options had vanished.

"And Phil?" Siobhan asked.

"Acknowledge in an hour, with whichever profanities seem most appropriate at the time," Heather replied.

Phil wouldn't have given an order like that unless he was serious. They needed to be able to run at the drop of a hat, with everyone aboard, so that *CS-405* wasn't crippled by crew shortages. *Packmule* could be a technical loss at that point, except Heather figured that Andre would be the first one gone, so they would either catch him at the first rendezvous, or he'd make it to Bok and those folks could escape.

Or cause more trouble themselves. It wasn't like they didn't have a good example in front of them already.

She turned and rose.

"Okay," she said to Kam and Markus. "Our priority just became the cutter. Yamaguchi will bring everyone here to help, but the crew in place needs to skip breakfast and naps and crash right back into work. Anybody not working on detaching the bow from the other ship and moving it to our cutter can go aboard number one and start prepping it for liftoff."

"Do we have a name for the cutter yet?" Markus

asked, almost as an aside as he turned and went down the stairs.

"I do," Heather called after him, over Kam's shoulder. "*Persephone.*"

"I don't get it," the engineer said. "Some literary reference?"

"Greek mythology, Markus," Kam said. "Bronze Age Earth."

"Correct," Heather said. "She was the daughter of Demeter, who was kidnapped by Hades, the god of the underworld. When she is eventually released, she becomes a goddess of the spring."

"I still don't get it," Markus said as he stepped into the airlock.

Kam followed and Heather triggered the lock mechanism

"*Buran* styles himself the *Lord of Winter*," Heather said to the engineer. "In ancient Russian, that's what *Buran* means. But his time is over, and *Persephone* is going to herald the spring."

PERSEPHONE (OCTOBER 14, 402)

THEY HAD ONLY BEEN GONE for about twenty minutes, but the look of surprise on their faces as they emerged from *Queen Anne's Revenge* was one Granville knew he would cherish. Captain Lau had put him in charge, and he had over a dozen folks with engineering backgrounds and strong backs, plus an understanding that something bad might have happened.

So he had put them to work.

Welders were adding rings and hooks to the forward section of ruined derelict number two. Another team had already cleared the cables connected to the removed bow of number one, and were stretching them out to reach the pulleys Galin had just finished attaching.

In a pinch, he would sacrifice the old bow, if that meant that they had a fourth ship, and one with guns.

Heather and Kam walked over and viewed things. Markus kept going, back to his truck, where it was obvious he would be needed far sooner than they had anticipated. Heather touched faceplates instead of using the radio.

"Siobhan is going over to the other site to retrieve the crew and Yamaguchi," she said. "Phil's ordered us to be ready to lift on two-minutes notice, so everybody is going to work here until your ship is ready."

"My ship?" Granville was surprised.

He was just getting used to the idea of being a shuttle pilot. Staid and somewhat dull, he supposed, but far more likely to come home than a hotshot fighter jock.

"Your ship," Heather repeated. "Sweat equity, and I need someone with combat experience commanding it. Doubly so if we come back to rescue everyone else over on that planet. They'll rally to an Imperial officer, and a man, faster than they will to Siobhan or I. The new Emperor can change their minds when they meet her. And I have no doubts she will, but that's next week and we're fighting a war today."

"Yes, sir," Granville felt himself snapping to. Old habits did indeed die hard.

"And she will have a name now, rather than a simple hull designation," Heather continued. "*Persephone*."

"Goddess of Spring and Queen of the Underworld," Granville felt the old knowledge bubble to the top of his mind from unmapped depths. "A formidable and dangerous foe."

"That's the plan," Heather said. "When Siobhan returns, everyone who is not attaching a new bow will be inside, powering things on and preparing her for flight."

"Roger that," Granville said. "Already have this crew in motion."

"I can see that, Centurion," she smiled. "Good job. This is why I want you commanding her."

"Aye aye."

"Now, get *Caravan* prepped for the next bit," Heather ordered. "Somewhere there is a fuse burning."

Granville saluted automatically, for the first time in seven years, and ran across the quad to his shuttle. His old shuttle.

That thing that had been his future, five minutes ago.

Preflight wasn't that necessary, as he had only powered the engines down to an idle state, and left all the onboard systems on a warm standby, so he didn't have to redo everything in six hours. The fuel that he would have burned in that time would have been negligible.

Now, it meant that he just had to touch all the gauges and confirm that everything was still on the beam.

"Galin, what is your status?" Heather suddenly called over the radio, bringing Granville back into the present tense.

She had walked to the middle of the quad again and was facing *Caravan* across about forty meters of open field.

"Last bolt turning now," Galin called. "Ten seconds to clear."

"Ground crew, confirm your cables," Heather said next.

"All cables free and ready, *Ground Control*," someone replied.

Granville knew everyone on this mission, but not by

voice alone on the radio. That would change quickly enough, though.

"Kam, you will have terminal guidance," Heather said. "What is your status?"

"Crane is in place," the Chief Engineer replied. "We are ready for the bow section to be put into alignment so we can guide it home."

"*Caravan*, what is your status?"

Granville triple-checked, because what was coming was that important.

"*Caravan* is green, Ground Control," he replied.

"Galin?"

"Last bolt free," the engineer replied. "I am departing the derelict now."

"*Caravan*," Heather said. "Come to a clean hover and line up on me."

Granville couldn't suppress the immense smile on his face as he powered the shuttle up and brought her into the air, an extension of his fingers and his will.

Like before, Heather guided him closer, standing in the middle of everything like a war goddess on a battlefield, as she moved all her pieces around slowly with her hands in an industrial ballet.

Cables attached. Elevation until they turned into violin strings. Markus in the Towtruck joining his symphony.

Hands off the joysticks, he directed the autopilot with single clicks, a pianist only slowly working his way up to Rachmaninoff from a cold, hungry, jazz intro.

This bow separated with only a little effort, perhaps

jarred loose in the same way that the other bow had been nearly welded in place.

In the background, *Queen Anne's Revenge* lifted off and slid across the plateau low and fast, a hawk seeking chickens rather than a shuttle going for orbit. Granville barely registered the ship's departure, except to note the dust she kicked up as a measure of the idle breezes outside.

So far, so good.

"*Caravan*, hold in place," Heather ordered.

He had the new bow pulled across the sand now, but they had done it so lightly that it trenched a line barely wider than his palm as they did. The repulsors hummed angrily, but their temperature held steady and the engines delivered smooth power.

On the underside camera, he saw Galin clambering over the vessel with new cables, running up to a pulley on the top hull of *Persephone*.

She had a name now. And a mission.

Shortly, a heartbeat.

The engineer did his esoteric magic with cables and geometry before running clear of the vessel. Nobody was safe, with this many tons of steel possibly rolling around, but unless a cable parted, he could protect his friends.

His *friends*.

Yes, he had truly come home.

Centurion Granville Veitengruber, *RAN*. Not even a flight centurion. But still an officer and a gentleman. And a commander of a cutter, if he wanted it bad enough.

And he did.

"*Caravan*," Heather said over the open line. "Bring it

up about fifteen centimeters and hold. Ground crews, keep all lines firm so that it does not swing."

Assents everywhere.

Granville took hold of the joysticks again. The computer wouldn't react as fast as his sense of touch, and harmonics would be worse than bad right now. If he let the bow section swing too hard, he could ruin both pieces and they would have to start over, possibly with a badly damaged vessel that they might only partially repair.

No, he wanted this warrior, this *Persephone*.

Fingertip pressure on the joystocks. Just a faintest lean into a breeze that was so light he thought he might have imagined it, except that the ship stayed aligned as he lifted.

"Kam?" Heather called.

"Stand by," the woman answered. "We're close but not aligned cleanly. Maybe as little as one centimeter low, clockwise side."

"Kam, this is *Caravan*," Granville said. "Everybody hold firm and stand by. I'll lift it."

"You'll need to rotate the piece in place, *Caravan*," Kam answered sharply. "We're on true with the beam."

"Roger that," he called. "Stand by for rotation counter-clockwise."

Deep breath. One centimeter of rotation in place, with cables that could stretch more than that under the load and part with too much stress from the shuttle overhead.

Granville heard the symphony play in his head. Found the note on the violin that the conductor wanted.

He closed his eyes and let his fingers play the note,

moving the insertion shuttle in six axes of motion at once: *X, Y, Z, Pitch, Roll, Yaw.*

The song changed. Granville felt it in his soul before the sound even made it as far as his fingers. He froze exactly in place, a single chip of diamond falling perfectly from the larger stone to render the last cut perfect.

"*Caravan*, hold there," Kam said an eternity later.

It had been less than a second, but Granville's soul was already running faster than his heart, almost JumpSpace speeds across the vastness of his imagination.

"Ground teams, board the derelict and start setting your sockets now," Heather called.

They had to be careful, not to knock the ship off the twenty pegs it was hanging on, but Granville smiled. He let the ship drift again, just enough to put weight on those twenty-centimeter bolts, and then hold them in place, pulling ever so slightly backwards to hold the two pieces in union.

On the camera, bodies ran towards the ship, impact hammers and prybars held out like swords and polearms for battle.

"*Caravan*, what is your status?" Heather asked.

"We are resting clean on the cables, Ground Control," he answered proudly.

"Can you lower yourself in place without torqueing?" she pressed.

"Affirmative."

"Good," Heather said. "Down one and forward one. I want to see it lean on the pegs, but I want you there to hold it if it slides."

It wouldn't slide, but he didn't tell Heather that. In

that last movement of the symphony, Granville was sure he heard *Persephone* herself awaken. She would hold everything now, while Galin and the others did their job.

The ship, this goddess *Persephone*, was ready to rejoin them on the surface, after a winter in hell. She could return to the land of the living.

As could Granville.

HOMEWARD BOUND (OCTOBER 18, 402)

GRANVILLE GRINNED as *Persephone* lifted high enough that the star cleared the horizon above them, a dawn in reverse.

"Engineering, everything looks good on my boards," he said into the internal comm.

She was running with a skeleton crew today, just in case something went wrong. Just him on the bridge, trying to handle everything, and Galin Tuason aft, watching the power systems. Between them, one of the engineers Granville had only met on this mission was monitoring life support.

"Engines appear to be holding," Galin replied. "Generators are badly out of tune, but we knew that and won't fix it here. JumpSails claim to be working normally, but we won't know until we try."

"Roger that, Galin," Granville smiled even broader as the ship pushed them higher and higher. "Life Support, what's your status?"

"All boards clean," Isiah replied. "Mix is a little rich, but I'm doing that on purpose, in case something breaks. With only three of us, that buys us an extra hour before we have to go into suits."

First-Rate-Spacer Isiah Olshefski. A farm boy from the suburbs of *Ladaux*, the beating heart of *Aquitaine*. Helping a former slave wage war for the *Empire*. His first crew, since Galin would go back to *Packmule* after this mission.

And the joke about suits wasn't idle. They had lived in them for more than a week on the surface, removing them only to have an occasional shower and reset the suits themselves. Even now, his helmet was attached to a hook on the console nearby, where it wouldn't float off if they lost power or grav-plates.

C-4268 had been down on *Three* for almost twenty years before it provided the stern two thirds of this vessel. *C-4711*'s bow had been there for eleven. Nobody was entirely sure how long everything would run before breaking, but they had taken time to strip parts off the other vessels and stuff them into *Caravan*'s containers.

Now they just had to make the run to *Lighthouse Station*.

"*Persephone*, this is Heather," her voice came over the comm.

Granville had never programmed a laser-link communication network, but he had experts who could, and it worked. That was good enough.

"Go ahead," he said.

"Everything looks good externally," she continued. "Prepare for orbital insertion."

"Roger that."

Granville checked his boards and sighed. Straight up, hold in place, and then jump clear when *Queen Anne's Revenge* joined them. On one screen, he could see *Caravan* climbing into orbit with them. Chief Engineer Rushforth had apparently been trained to fly vessels like that at one point, and volunteered when they had more vessels than pilots. She and Heather were trailing them to orbit, where *Saddlebags* had already docked with *Packmule*.

"All vessels, this is Phil," the admiral joined them now. "Double broach complete and Evan confirms that the solar system is clear. *Queen Anne*, start your ascent."

CS-405 had just done something so amazing Granville still got chills thinking about the orbital geometry necessary.

While the corvette stayed in the shadow of *Three*, relative to *Mansi-B*, Captain Kosnett had drifted far enough sideways that they could see the backside of *Mansi-D,*. There had been a very slim chance that the Hammerhead had been bluffing about its departure, and had instead slipped into the one blind spot *CS-405* had, from which the Hammerhead could hop around the gas giant and ambush the squadron.

Granville had seen the cone of various sensor shadows projected and overlapping, and he would have thought it was too small for his old fighter craft to fit into and remain hidden, let alone a corvette. But the Science Officer and the Admiral knew their stuff.

And he was one of them now.

Just as *Persephone* was.

"Galin, make sure we're charged, and prepare for

transition to JumpSpace," Granville said. "Next stop, *Lighthouse Station*."

ABOUT THE AUTHOR

Blaze Ward writes science fiction in the Alexandria Station universe (Jessica Keller, The Science Officer, The Story Road, etc.) as well as several other science fiction universes, such as Star Dragon, the Collective, and more. He also writes odd bits of high fantasy with swords and orcs. In addition, he is the Editor and Publisher of *Boundary Shock Quarterly Magazine*. You can find out more at his website www.blazeward.com, as well as Facebook, Goodreads, and other places.

Blaze's works are available as ebooks, paper, and audio, and can be found at a variety of online vendors (Kobo, Amazon, and others). His newsletter comes out quarterly, and you can also follow his blog on his website. He really enjoys interacting with fans, and looks forward to any and all questions—even ones about his books!

Never miss a release!
If you'd like to be notified of new releases, sign up for my newsletter.

I will never spam you or use your email for nefarious purposes. You can also unsubscribe at any time.

http://www.blazeward.com/newsletter/

Connect with Blaze!

Web: www.blazeward.com
Boundary Shock Quarterly (BSQ):
https://www.boundaryshockquarterly.com/

facebook.com/KRPBlaze

goodreads.com/Blaze_Ward

ABOUT KNOTTED ROAD PRESS

Knotted Road Press fiction specializes in dynamic writing set in mysterious, exotic locations.

Knotted Road Press non-fiction publishes autobiographies, business books, cookbooks, and how-to books with unique voices.

Knotted Road Press creates DRM-free ebooks as well as high-quality print books for readers around the world.

With authors in a variety of genres including literary, poetry, mystery, fantasy, and science fiction, Knotted Road Press has something for everyone.

Knotted Road Press
www.KnottedRoadPress.com